**Ms. Alignec**

publishec

We thank the following for generously donating to make this publication possible.

Mary-Kim Arnold
Suzanne Casart
Stacey Crandall
Katherine Dering
Michelle Diffenderfer
Katharine Duane
Phyllis Dull
Naomi Long Eagleson
El León Literary Arts
Frankie Enos
Derek Frerichs
Martina Freund
Chelsea Gelson
Stephanie Han
Tracie Hara
Dwight Hilson
Ken Herndon
Lillian Howan
Min Jung
Ghada Khalil
Priscilla Kalugdan
Caroline Kim-Brown
Ranah Matott LeBouf
Susan Levin
John LoSasso
Maura Macdarmada
Diana Mankaruse
Mānoa Foundation
Serena and Kendra Matott
Pat Matsueda
Alan Mawyer
Sharon May
Jonathan Morse
Emilya Naymark
Sabrina Noah
Carolo O'Brien
Connie Pan
Ann Pancake
Adam and Tara Patten
Emmy Laybourne Podunovich
Grace Loh Prasad
Vanessa Reaves
Ashley Saucedo
Michael Schmicker
Jill Schoenmehl
Ron Schoenmehl
Victoria Totaro
Marianne Villanueva
E. Wilder
Olga Zilberbourg

Detail from *Old Country, Syria* by Melissa Chimera

# ms. aligned

## 3

### Women Writing About Men


Rebecca Thomas
*Editor*

Pat Matsueda
*Founder*



El León Literary Arts
*Berkeley*

Mānoa Books
*Honolulu*

Published 2020 by
El León Literary Arts of Berkeley, California (elleonliteraryarts.org)
and Mānoa Books of Honolulu, Hawai'i (manoafoundation.org)



Front-cover art and frontispiece *Old Country, Syria* by Melissa Chimera
Back-cover art *Hurricane* by Carly Elizabeth Huggins

Production by
Noah Perales-Estoesta
Peak Services (peakserviceshawaii.com)

ISBN 978-0-9799504-2-1
Printed in the United States of America

# Contents

# Editor's Note

## Rebecca Thomas

For the past nine years, I have been teaching composition at West Virginia University. I primarily teach freshmen, and one of their first papers is a narrative. In so many of the narratives, students—of all genders—explore issues connected to masculinity, in particular the effects of toxic masculinity. I receive papers about abusive relationships in high school, peer pressure to act a certain way, loneliness in emotionally connecting with peers, and the very real risk and fallout from coming out. My students are young, so it's natural that they write about their childhood, the fragile moments where they begin to construct their identity. In our class discussions and in their reflections, I see so many grappling with the concept of masculinity. How did it shape their life? How will it shape their life as they journey into adulthood?

In this Me Too era, it's hard not to think about masculinity and how it can be toxic. Working on a college campus, I know that many of my students have been assaulted, I know that many of them are trying to find the space to talk about it, and I know that many of them are starting to test the waters of self-acceptance, to see if it is safe to be who they are. Since I am the mother of two young boys, toxic masculinity is something that I have to consider constantly: how do we raise our children in this environment? What conversations do I need to have with my kids? What tools can I provide them, so they don't end up with narratives like so many of my students?

The work in this book addresses these questions. As we've started to shift the global conversation into accepting multiple forms of masculinity, the work supports these notions: there is no one type of childhood and there is no one way to be a "boy." Although these works take on widely diverse viewpoints and experiences, they remind us of the vulnerability of childhood, of that stretch of time as we begin to find who we are and who others want us to be.

In the pages of *Ms. Aligned 3*, we see the struggle as children try to form identities outside of their parents and try to understand where their place is alongside their caregivers. Ryane Nicole Granados's excerpt "Star Cruiser" illustrates what it means to have an absent father, to navigate how to talk about fathers who are not there, and to come to terms with our own relationship to them. Marilyn Stablein's "Isthmus," Caroline Kim's "The Prince of Mournful Thoughts," and Marianne Villanueva's "Dumaguete," explore the tension that comes from children trying to find their place between parents and of the conflict that arises when children don't live up to parental expectations. Villanueva takes gender roles head on as her protagonist, a boy on the cusp of adolescence, tries to find his place between loyalties and longing for both his mother and father. She reminds us of the silence that children, especially males, often learn because of their parents, writing, "he always felt he knew how to hide his emotions. It was a skill his mother lacked, and he had realized this about her very early. And he had carefully tended to his face, even when he was startled, even when he felt lost." It is moments like these that I realize the impact that the work in this anthology has. We see the interior of these characters; we see the depth of emotions that we often forget—or ignore—from young children, especially boys. As is the case in all great literature, by exploring the specifics of one character's relationship, we gain better understandings of our own relationships to our parents, to ourselves, and to childhood, too.

Likewise, I was drawn to the work that explores versions of motherhood: what does it mean to decide to raise a child, such as Gerda Govine Ituarte's "Boy Dancing" and Grace Loh Prasad's "Teddy"? Conversely, in Pat Matsueda's stunning poem, "To My Unborn Son," what does it mean to decide not to? What responsibilities do we have as we bring our children into the world? What are the ways we can usher them into a sense of themselves?

Furthermore, these works help us understand the connection of vulnerability and budding sexuality. Angela Nishimoto's memoir excerpt, "Sex Education: A Tragicomedy, Part II," explores the strength children need when they encounter the social boundaries of gender and race. We are transported to our first unrequited loves and the cost of staying silent with Connie Pan's poem "Want in the Third Grade." Pan reminds us of the depth of feeling every child has, even if adults dismiss it, when she writes about the pang of longing for an ex's best friend: "The way you looked/into me glittered my everything, but/you couldn't because *loyalty.* I can taste/that eight-year-old regret, remember/the mourning. What a tiny kill." Reading this poem, I remember those loves so deep, those hidden diary scrawls, and the very real feelings I had, even if adults often find those feelings "cute."

I see the vulnerability of "boyhood" especially in the work that explores children trying to make sense of the world. Lillian Howan's "The Blue Medium" follows an adolescent boy, an apprentice, as he tries to do the seemingly impossible (especially for a young boy): lose himself and become fully present. Mary Carozza's "Keys" follows a young piano prodigy who is returning to stage after two horrible performances. Rachel King's "CD Player" gives us a story of a teenager processing the grief of his mother's terminal illness through the music of Elliot Smith. She gives us that glimpse into the universal teenage experience of having music name our feelings through a distinctly teenage voice: "The sound was everything I was feeling and had felt, for as long as I could remember having feelings." As readers, we are reminded of the very real danger that kids can find themselves in when they try to navigate the world of adults on their own in Donna Lee Miele's "Crocodile Teeth." In Jeannine Ouellette's work, "Family, Family," she tells the story of a first grader who creates his own baby made of yarn. We feel the keen sense of risk in being the "different" one: "The children, being children, were nonetheless bloodthirsty, and stiffened in anticipation of the kill—cheeks bright with the heat of the afternoon, fingers sticky with honey—as all around us, swerving drunkenly through the air and in the dry grass, came the bees, golden and heavy with the change of seasons, wings glinting in the thin light, stingers ready, mouths searching." Through these works, I am transported to my own childhood, to the wonder of discovery, the yearning for connection, and the desire to have someone also understand what I was going through. I will hold on to this anthology as I help usher my boys through childhood.

After reading the first two anthologies and seeing those fabulous writers' take on the male gaze, I was so interested to see how we could look at the vulnerability of males as boys. How would the perspective shift? What can we learn to create a more empathetic world? From a selfish standpoint, I needed to read this work for the sake of my students and my children. In Ann Pancake's wonderful interview, she gives the following advice to budding writers: "I would recommend that the young writers step outside themselves—put the self off to the side—and climb into the body, the mind, and the heart of the male character." She reminds us to "take risks. Stay open to what your characters are showing you. Listen. Don't impose your self." For me, this is the heart of what the Ms. Aligned series does: we step inside another perspective to gain a deeper understanding of our world.

**ACKNOWLEDGEMENTS**

Working on Ms. Aligned these past two editions has highlighted the wonderful generosity of fellow artists. Fellow Ms. Aligned board members, Connie Pan and Lillian Howan, have been beyond generous with their time in all stages of this process and in providing their keen editorial insight. The emails for this edition have spanned years, and both women have been remarkably patient and enthusiastic as they helped shape this anthology. I am still in awe that we have Shawna Yang Ryan's wonderful introduction and

Ann Pancake's fantastic interview. I catch myself staring at the beautiful art from Melissa Chimera and Carly Huggins. And I greatly appreciate the hard work that Noah Perales-Estoesta put into early design of the book.

The early support from Thomas Farber of El León Literary Arts made the first conversations about this anthology happen, and his continued support, along with that of Frank Stewart, of Mānoa Foundation, allowed this book to come into the world.

The incredible generosity from our Kickstarter supporters has been humbling. With backers from all over the country—and the world—it has been remarkable to see such an outpouring of support. I also want to thank Carrie Slimak for handcrafting the mugs that were part of this fundraiser.

Finally, the Ms. Aligned series is first and foremost Pat Matsueda's baby. It has been such an honor working with her and having her trust me in this editorial role. She has worked tirelessly alongside me, soliciting, editing, typesetting, designing, writing, interviewing, tweeting, and fundraising. To say that this edition wouldn't exist without Pat is an understatement. It has been a gift working with and learning from Pat. Thank you.

REBECCA THOMAS's fiction and nonfiction have appeared in *Prairie Schooner, Hunger Mountain, The Massachusetts Review, Fifth Wednesday,* and other journals. In 2015, she received a Pushcart Prize nomination for fiction. She received her MFA in creative writing from West Virginia University. She received undergraduate degrees in creative writing and screenwriting from Chapman University. Originally from Orange County, California, she now teaches writing in Morgantown, West Virginia.

# Introduction

**Shawna Yang Ryan**

Gendering starts in the womb; when I was pregnant, it was the first question people would ask me—even my most progressive colleagues who taught gender and queer studies: "Are you having a boy or girl?" I wanted to answer, cheekily, "Well, the baby is genetically male, but we won't know their gender for a while."

Before my son was born, I decided I wanted to dress him in "gender-neutral" clothes. In conversation with Stephen Colbert, Billy Porter, the Emmy-winning actor from the show *Pose,* made a powerful comment about gender and clothing:

> Women wearing pants is powerful, it's strong, everybody accepts it, and it's associated with the patriarchy. It's associated with being male. The minute a man puts on a dress it's disgusting. So what are you saying? Men are strong, women are disgusting. I'm not doing that anymore. I'm done with that. I'm a man in a dress, and if I feel like wearing a dress, I'm going to wear one.

In the children's clothing section, "gender neutral" means gray or black-and-white. Green and yellow have been claimed by the gender binary, as have animals. Dinosaurs and dogs are for "boys"; cats and unicorns are for "girls" (though boys get the big cats: tigers and lions). I cringed at my complicity in the gendering process every time I put my son in a shirt decorated with dump trucks or baseballs. I told myself that if my son's wardrobe wasn't "neutral," it could at least be fluid, and yet, thinking of the potential remarks from my family (or strangers) and feeling the deep-seated, reflexive way I'd been socialized to traditional expressions of gender, I hesitated at buying a flowered or ruffled onesie. Was I making a statement for my own sake? Would wearing a sparkly unicorn shirt as a three-month-old help my son defy gender norms as an adult?

I knew, intellectually, that gendering is a lifelong process, composed of constant small and large pressures, but now I saw it in a concrete way. The broader questions weighed on me: How can I raise a son who will evade the cult of (toxic) masculinity? What does it mean to be a "man"? Lines from Don

DeLillo's *White Noise* came to mind: "These were the things that built the world. Not to know or care about them was a betrayal of fundamental principles, a betrayal of gender, of species. What could be more useless than a man who couldn't fix a dripping faucet—fundamentally useless, dead to history, to the messages in his genes?" This encapsulated the pressures my son would face. Defying the expectations of traditional masculinity was "a betrayal." *The message in his genes.*

An experiment: what does a search of quotes tagged "masculinity" on the site Goodreads.com—an unofficial survey of what readers have pulled from the 2.6 billion books reviewed there—reveal about how masculinity is written about and perceived? What lines have struck the 90 million site users strongly enough to be highlighted and tagged? Scanning these quotes discloses a vision of masculinity that is complex, multifaceted, and much discussed in works ranging from the academic to poetry. However, some recurring themes emerge, many of them revolving around "toxic masculinity": a concept rooted in violence, in power, and in seeking and suppressing pain. A masculinity that sets itself in opposition to femininity (and feminism!), that fears femininity, or considers it disgusting. For example, in this jarring line, Patton Oswalt combines the disgust and the violence with humorous intent: "I had a romance novel inside me, but I paid three sailors to beat it out of me with steel pipes."

What changes when masculinity is imagined and portrayed by women? In the third volume of the *Ms. Aligned* series, the editors and writers continue the project of exploring—as board member Lillian Howan puts it—"the intersection between female creator and male creation." Volume three focuses on childhood. These pieces, as a collection, ask, How do boys become men? How does the narrative of masculinity develop? And what is that narrative?

The *Ms. Aligned* series originated in the vision of writer and editor Pat Matsueda, who sought to trouble the gender binary by upending the traditional narrative dynamic and offering depictions of men through the female gaze. Since volume one, the *Ms. Aligned* editors have striven to question our preconceived notions of how others see the world, whether it's women looking through the eyes of men, or adults seeing through the eyes of children.

In a creative writing class, an instructor might offer the exercise to "write from the point of view of a child," as if "childhood" was a single perspective. The pieces in *Ms. Aligned 3* demonstrate that a child's point of view is as singular and unique as the adult they grow into. From a range of authors diverse in geographical location, experiences, and style, the prose and poems in this anthology offer a rich variety of perspectives. Portrayed with empathy, pathos, and unexpected narrative twists, common themes surface: yearning for parental approval/guidance/presence (Ryane Nicole Granados's "Star Cruiser";

Rachel King's "CD Player"; Caroline Kim's "The Prince of Mournful Thoughts"; Marilyn Stablein's "Isthmus"), adults failing children (Marianne Villanueva's "Dumaguete"), anxiety and loneliness (Grace Loh Prasad's "Teddy"; Mary Carozza's "Keys"). Pieces such as Jeannine Ouelette's "Family, Family" and Gerda Govine Ituarte's "Boy Child" speak in the voice of adults worrying over what kind of men young boys might become. Pat Matsueda's devastating poem "To My Unborn Son" addresses the child that never was. Other pieces tackle timely social issues, such as the border detention camps in Rebecca Thomas's "Milestones" and addiction in Mary Archer's "Desolation Row." Irony and poignancy arise from the dissonance between adult understanding and child experience, such as in Angela Nishimoto's "Sex Education: A Tragicomedy, Part II," Donna Lee Miele's "Crocodile Teeth," and Connie Pan's "Want in the Third Grade." Lastly, Lillian Howan's "The Blue Medium" offers a luminous, moody look at a boy's life on the precipice of manhood.

This is a collection about looking and seeing and the attempt to understand how the adult world functions and how innocence is lost. This collection makes a critical contribution to the conversation about masculinity as it forces readers, by transporting us back to childhood, to confront how we have all been complicit or conditioned into the roles that uphold the society we live in. This volume of *Ms. Aligned* offers just the right words for our times.

---

**SHAWNA YANG RYAN** is a former Fulbright scholar and the author of *Water Ghosts* (Penguin Press, 2009) and *Green Island* (Knopf, 2016). She is the director of the creative writing program at the University of Hawai'i at Mānoa. Her writing has appeared in *ZYZZYVA*, the *Asian American Literary Review*, the *Rumpus*, *Lithub*, and the *Washington Post*. Her work has received the Association for Asian American Studies Best Book Award in in Creative Writing, the Eilliot Cades Emerging Writer Award, and an American Book Award.

*Hurricane* by Carly Elizabeth Huggins

# Desolation Row

**Mary Archer**

*After the 2005 documentary* Dope Sick Love

Amber streetlight shining
like electric setting sun
hung perpetual like
a cut of forever warmth

He is alone, slung deliberate
over graffitied post office box,
shirtless in this spring
or summer night,
or fall

Dusky light encounters contours
of a once youthful cheek
then fourteen, now twenty, or thirty,
or as old as time
as old as the streets

Chin too young
to be this sunken,
muscles, abs and arms
lonely in their skin—
a straight man's wares
angling in any "trick"
who knows
exactly what he gets

Sheared blond hair
and eyes a stormy blue-gray

placid like ocean
after torrential rain;
jeans just shy of baggy
for this frame,
held close by a belt
like a cheap fix
of some saving grace

Hey Matt,
when did you join the ranks
of needle-thin people
our memories have jostled together
on that dark street corner
we each name
in silence?

Matt, is your neat
expression of desolation
carefully fitted
to each shadowy figure
wandering your way?

Which part is you
and which part is you trying
to look "lonely and pathetic"?
So sharp, your girlfriend Tracy answers:
looking on in the dark deep
across the street,
she easily sees
your difference

That line you say you crossed
when there was no turning back,
when the lifestyle has you locked—
was the line clocked at age twelve
at the Garden, Madison Square
where your busy innocence scalped tickets

and upsold concert arena highs for higher
or was that line boarded at age thirteen
downtown at Penn Station
"sweet talking people out of their money"?
Or did the line float
with the hustle and the con, snaking
all the way down
to Greenwich Village,
hustling at age fourteen?

Buzzing light flickering briefly
—the night has no takers
so your girlfriend suggests you drop a line
to two old gays looking for a good time
Agreeing, you skip to call,
holding your wayward pants up

Their incandescent light flooding past
rickety apartment doorway beam
giving shape to all your promise
naked in full view,
your jeans pooled on the floor
like storming waves of denim blue

After, you hug and smile and kiss him
wishing each other good night
his lover watching coolly
naked beneath his sheets
You part like friends
like a gift was given you

Going to see your mom in Jersey
Before you board you shoot dope
in a bathroom stall at Old Navy
You flick toilet water drawn
into your used syringe

to clean it, solemn,
because you won't do drugs around your mother
Because it would kill her

Bus window wiping scene to scene,
telephone wire and concrete street
Red brick building after building
to a wide low sky and great oak trees
Remembering smoking angel dust, age eleven,
by the tombstones gathered at West Side Cemetery
Was this the gateway to your gateway?

Looking up and pointing,
a two-story building with horizontal gray slats
Your dad did all the aluminum siding, you say proudly
He died of a heart attack a couple months ago
Growing up you remember
your block was "the only white block"
You walk past
waving to a black kid your age
just a brief lifetime ago
But you "grew up here and love it"

Your mom welcomes you, smiling fiercely,
asking for money so the dream house she bought
on the same block she can't seem to get off
can get paid for in another thirty years
You show pictures and make cereal which
sloshes over the shallow blue plastic bowl and say
"don't cry over spilt milk"

Your mom says you were a good kid
abrupt noise and a smooth needle
A car crash at age twelve had
wiped your memory clean like a clock hand
winding back to zero
or so you had said

*Matt City,* a composite digital illustration by Pat Matsueda. Incorporated are images from *Dope Sick Love* and maps of Manhattan and the train route from New York to New Jersey.

Matt, I hear you're doing better now
have a child with your girlfriend
have an apartment where
the door opens with the twist
of your key instead of the slide
of a credit card, opening
some building's door
because you want safely
to get smacked

You and Tracy have made
desolation row the shit of paradise,
thrusting up green shoots
of hope and everything lost
like middle fingers to concrete
voyaging to sunlight

Matt, the two of you kiss
like Adam and Eve after rehab,
sharing smoke kisses and words
that this "isn't a whim," as Tracy says—
not to please her father
but is what you both want

Her dad gave you so many sweaters
your closet is a cloud of yarn,
and stacks
of DVDs, forty or fifty, and more each time
Matt, is this how you get high now—
video games and movies for $1.99?

## AUTHOR'S STATEMENT

The 2005 HBO documentary *Dope Sick Love* follows two drug-addicted couples around Manhattan, New York City, and locations in New Jersey. One couple is Matt and Tracy, both Caucasian cocaine and heroin users in their late twenties or early thirties who are looking to get out of their "rough life-style[s]" with the help of Tracy's supportive father. Their story is told over an eighteen-month period in a bare-bones style without interview questions, narration, or exposition. Startled by the often graphic images, candid drug use, and the frank, open warmth of Matt, I wrote this poem as a way of trying to piece together what he had to show or say.

Growing up in Staten Island, a suburban middle-class borough in NYC, I was attending middle school at the time this documentary came out. I wasn't familiar with the "crack epidemic" of the early 1980s and 1990s except through watching bits and pieces of reruns of *Chappelle's Show* on Comedy Central. But like other kids, I was vaguely aware that "crackheads"—men and women under the influence of crack cocaine—were damaged, unpredictable people I should stay away from. Today I know that the epidemic occurred largely in inner-city areas in the northeast, and that NYC, Newark, and Philadelphia had the highest indexes of incidents related to crack cocaine.

Matt, a native of New Jersey but a local of NYC, is shown picking apartment building locks with Tracy in order to get high. He's a contradictory, sometimes sweet, sometimes blunt individual who grew up in what he calls "the ghetto, the slums." I believe he has strong, positive ties to his old neighborhood—not only because of the snippets we see but also because throughout the film, he is shown having an unusual camaraderie with people: Tracy, his mother, Tracy's father, the taxi driver, the boy sitting on the stoop, the prostitution clients. (He isn't shown accepting any money, but we understand he offers sexual favors ultimately to purchase drugs. Some part of his income may go to helping his mother with her mortgage.) Contrasted with Sebastian and Michelle, the other drug-addicted couple the documentary follows, Matt has made the very best of his situation and the strongest relationship foundation. The other couple's relationships crumble in increasing isolation and dysfunction.

Growing up is an ugly thing. It is both a shocking and sensitizing process as one begins to understand the horror and the gift that is life. The gift that is offered Matt is the barest gift, and heaviest: choice. Becoming self-determining is growing up, but no one tells you how fraught with trouble and laden with grace the process is.

**MARY ARCHER** is a University of Hawaiʻi at Mānoa graduate with a baccalaureate in English. Her writing has appeared in the two previous editions of *Ms. Aligned: Women Writing About Men.* A poetry suite dedicated to Robert McHenry, a professor of English at the University of Hawaiʻi at Mānoa, appeared in the inaugural edition of *Ms. Aligned.* In the second edition, she published a short fiction work, "Death of Blossom Girl." In spring 2015, her essay and narrative fiction piece appeared in *Ka Hue Anahā: Journal of Academic & Research Writing,* Kapiʻolani Community College's student periodical. She is a New York native and current Hawaiʻi local.

# Keys

## Mary Carozza

Deep breath in, out. Feel chest expand on the inhale, pause, count. Slowly exhale all the way, pause, count.

Marius looked down at his hands resting on his lap. His fingernails were short. He had no cuts, no hangnails. The sore tendon on the pinkie side of his left hand had healed nicely.

His eyes shifted up, focusing briefly on the bare white wall in the small, chilly practice room. The old upright had a musty smell—or it was the room itself. He shifted his weight back and forth on the bench and, placing hands on keys, began to go through the first piece one last time before heading to the anteroom. One last time before performing. The music was a short, simple composition, beginning with the slightly undecided, irregular heartbeat of the underlying rhythm: soft tones that take on clear contours throughout the piece but that, however, shouldn't be showcased—a continual fluctuation of chords to support the melody, to form the basis for the main voice that wouldn't begin to sound until the fourth bar, slipping in softly, gently asserting its singing timbre.

For this performance, Marius and his teacher had chosen an easier piece to begin—really, an easy piece—but one that highlighted his ability to interpret meaning and convey emotion. Here, the emotion was falling in love, the teller yielding totally and utterly to the adored one over the course of the short composition: At your feet, *For dine fötter* in the original Norwegian. Marius loved the piece, composed as it was with confident simplicity and suffused with touching harmonies, unorthodox phrases and arcs. It should be a joy to perform.

*Should be.* He paused in his play and tried to push away the memory of his last two performances, the first just a rare poor concert, the second an utter disaster in a big competition. He had never before fallen victim to such nerves. He had started his piece, a virtuoso Liszt, with a flurry of wrong notes. The errors overwhelmed him, and he could think of nothing but making up for them—he desperately wanted to make them forgotten. In the process, he lost his composure. He managed another minute or two before jumping up and running off the stage, out of the building, into the air, where he kept running, not stopping until he felt the vomit in his throat. His stomach heaved and he watched his breakfast splash onto the pavement, some specks landing on his black shoes and trousers. He realized he was at the city park, deserted at that time of day and year, and he went to a bench and sat for what felt like hours, his pile of vomit still in view. Just before his teacher found him, a crow came to pick at the parts that were still edible.

"Marius! Here you are!" She sat down next to him, placing her hand lightly on his arm. His mouth opened to reply, but no sound came out. Hot tears in his eyes, red spots on his cheeks. He opened and closed his soundless mouth a second time.

"Marius, let's go back. Everybody is looking for you. There will be another chance. Don't think too much about it."

When younger, he had never thought about performing at all. He played and people loved it. His nerves had begun bothering him only of late, after he turned 14, when he shifted from playing notes to interpreting music, to portraying his own ideas and impressions. He began feeling shy and unsure. With his new shyness came a fear that he might disappoint his listeners, that he would lose the goodwill shown to a young prodigy. A wunderkind, they called him: a child wonder. Earlier, it made him proud. But he was no longer a child, and he had begun to feel hostile towards an audience that simply sat there, listening and judging. The powerful passivity of his listeners struck him as hugely unjust.

His body was also doing strange things. He couldn't figure out how high to set the piano stool, how close to sit to the piano. It seemed that his bones and muscles were constantly moving, poking, prodding. His larger hands were an advantage, but he always needed to adjust something, to change, to figure out what to change. Just playing—*playing*—as he had as a young boy...He no longer knew how.

Sitting on the park bench with his teacher, he felt the tears roll over his hot cheeks. "I hate this," he choked. "I hate this."

His teacher patted his arm, then took his elbow. "Don't think too much about it, Marius."

A sharp knock at the door brought Marius's mind back to the practice room and the upcoming performance: He would be on stage in 15 minutes. His hot shame at the memory glowed on his cheeks as he left the small room and walked down the brightly lit corridor toward the anteroom, his shoes clicking on the brittle linoleum.

His teacher had been supportive over the past weeks. He knew he was more fortunate than many. He knew firsthand of the horror stories—teachers telling their protégés they would never amount to anything, calling them lazy and worthless. His teacher would change the fingering on a piece a few days before a competition, causing him no small confusion. And sometimes he wasn't sure if she was allowing him to interpret a piece or making him play how she wanted it. But she was clever and kind, and he trusted her. For today's performance, they had put together a charming portfolio of Grieg's lyrical pieces. It was nothing he could play at a tough competition, but this concert wasn't top tier. There was even a mix of instruments. The event was more a presentation of the conservatory's young talent than the high-level competitions and concerts he normally took part in. He knew his teacher chose it so he could regain some confidence.

He tried to push away the panicked thought that today his destiny would be decided. That if he failed today, he would be a failure.

Walking down the hall, Marius stopped to look through the glass door of a practice room and watched four flutists rehearsing their pieces in the same room, each musician facing the wall so as to be able to hear their own instrument and shut out all other sounds and impressions.

Upon reaching the small anteroom, he tried to ignore the other musicians as they tapped and shuffled their feet along the dry wooden floorboards, keeping time *(ta-ta-tatata, ta-ta-tatata, ta-ta-tatatata!)*. He tried to shut out the rustling as they sifted through sheet music and sang semi-tuneless rhythms *(la-la-lalala, la-la-lalala, la-la-lalalala!)*. The room's temperature was comfortable, and he was grateful not to have to worry about keeping his hands warm. He tried to tune out the constrictions in his gut as he mentally went through the first piece, seeking focus and concentrating his mind, not thinking about the audience or even about himself.

He heard his name called. It was time.

Practice lifted him to his feet and carried him out to the grand in the middle of the stage—there is always a golden sheen to the lighting in concert halls, and Marius paused a moment to note the peculiar shimmer and the reflection of a light or two on the sleek black surface of the instrument. He moved to the front of the stage and made a slight bow of acknowledgement, his eyes fixed at a spot in the back of the room where no one sat—or where he couldn't see if anyone sat—and then took his seat at the piano, part of him striving to concentrate, part of him thrilling to the opportunity to portray the music he loved. Again, it was his training that led him to shift his weight and find the right position for his body while something in the back of his memory reminded him to breathe. In and out. *At your feet.* He closed his eyes, listening in his mind to the heartbeat of the music, swaying his head from side to side with a barely perceptible motion. He thought of the blend of tension and relaxation his hands required to navigate the keys. He thought of proper elbow motion, of keeping his growing hands close to the keys. Opening his eyes, he lifted his left hand and began with the open chord, the heartbeat. He was slightly surprised by the sound. After having imagined it so clearly in his mind, hearing the rich tones with his ears seemed uncanny, yet beautifully so. He then lifted his right hand and began the simple, clear melody on top of the mesmerizing carpet of the underlying rhythm. He continued through the piece, portraying the composer's devotion, initially hesitant, then growing more certain, enjoying the sweet harmonies, shifting into the stringent, pleading intermediate part, and savoring the gorgeous, undulating chords that ache to be resolved at the end of the piece.

Upon finishing, he turned to his audience and bowed his head.

Maybe this was enough.

---

**AUTHOR'S STATEMENT**

The idea behind writing "Keys" was the desire to write about Edvard Grieg's "At Your Feet," a short lyrical piece composed for the piano that I was playing at the time. In my hearing, the music is a beautiful and sincere portrayal of devotion. It's the floating, gossamer-like depiction of being at the service of music, of art, of a loved one that I was curious to explore. It was my intention to find a verbal and narrative portrayal of the music's devotion, if not of devotion itself.

Then a boy showed up to play the piece for me. He quickly had a name (it's only writing this that I see the similarity with my own), and I had a familiar thought: how odd that my protagonist was, as in so much of my writing, male. Although my most recent texts focus on girls and women, most of my stories—and nearly all my earliest pieces—have been about a man or a boy: an unnamed traveler, a kindly neighbor, a circus director, a clown…Despite the high population density of men in my stories, I still haven't got used to it, and it always triggers a slight feeling of unease as well as a sense of puzzlement. I question my right to write about boys and men. After all—though I've had a father, brother, son, various relationships, schoolmates, bosses, neighbors—what do I know about being male? And isn't one of the first rules of writing that we should write about what we know?

Part of my unease with writing about men is related to culture and gender. Men have, of course, always written about women, and this naturally has had wide, far-ranging consequences for women and men alike. From the men who wrote—and interpreted—the Bible, on to Defoe's Moll Flanders, Richardson's Pamela and Camilla, Dickens's Dora, Hardy's Tess, even Shaw's Mrs. Warren: male writers and thinkers have depicted female figures and thus shaped how society perceives women and their role in the world. Saint or whore. Whore with a heart of gold. Victim. Maidservant. Feminist with a character flaw. And this makes me wonder: Have I instinctively veered towards male characters because they aren't weighted down by these stereotypical roles? Because they are free agents?

My un-ease perhaps also stems from a worry that—even if I'm not a widely read author—I could be unwittingly perpetuating existing male stereotypes. Or that I'm perhaps unknowingly proposing a new type of male character. And if the latter is true, is this new type something that could lead to a better, fairer society? Or is it a negative stereotype that would, in the end, harm us all—just as I'm certain the female characters developed by men have not always been conducive to a positive societal development. (Not to put too fine a point on it: it's a tough fate to be a saint, a whore, or a victim.)

Another reason that my many male protagonists puzzle me is simply that I've never wanted to be a boy or a man—I'm quite pleased to be female—and yet I identify very closely with my male figures on an emotional level, something that's not always the case with my female protagonists. When I write about women, they are without exception portrayed as coming to terms with the world around them, negotiating and navigating society as they find it—and I think it's generally fair to say that it's still a man's world (heads of state, CEOs, leaders at universities, etc.). It's also fair to say that I am very much aware of gender roles; it's something I think of and speak about frequently. So why don't I consciously explore the male gaze and the situation of men and boys in this world when I write about males? Shouldn't I be asking specifically what it is to be male in a given context?

Of course, hyper-awareness of underlying motives and possible effects might be a lot to expect and even more to require—both of ourselves and of others. Practicing such heightened consciousness as an author is also probably a certain way to keep oneself from ever putting a single word to paper...And in the end, I think we have no choice other than to write about what we know—even when we're dealing with boy pianists and male circus directors.

So all I can do is tread with caution and have a good deal of respect when writing my male protagonists. Yet, although I've certainly nothing against the idea of exploring the male gaze, being male in the world is not my main interest in the stories these characters feature in. My interest in them is individual—how they navigate their lives, their dreams—not in society but in their own personal, emotional, interior worlds. And my stories, too, are individual, personal, interior. I begin to suspect that adopting a male point-of-view helps me to step back from my own self and from the strong ego that dictates and controls what I should think, feel, and write. And that this "foreign" perspective leads me over new, less cluttered pathways to clearer insights. One thing is certain: had I written about me—or a girl—playing "At Your Feet," an entirely different narrative would have unfolded, one that was ten times as complex and, possibly, a thousand times more muddled. So—considered under a microscope—while it seems rather audacious to write about a man without considering his manhood and perhaps careless, even callous, to write about a boy like Marius without explicitly considering his boyhood, there it is. Marius, a boy on the threshold to manhood, helped me to freely and non-judgmentally explore how we perform, how we are at the service of our medium yet not servile. How we can be present and still. And how it's possible that maybe, just maybe, that's enough.

MARY CAROZZA is a translator and writer living near Zurich, Switzerland. Originally from the Midwest, she holds an undergraduate degree in German studies and a graduate degree in English and creative writing. Her translations have appeared in various scholarly journals and art publications. In her writing, she explores themes of otherness and belonging.

# Star Cruiser: 1988

**Ryane Nicole Granados**

My father is an astronaut, a moonwalker, a star cruiser. Prose and I are the daughters of a rocket-riding explorer. When we were young, he left on a top-secret mission. He said, "I'll be back. Don't wait up. I'm off to save the world." Mercy swears he didn't say the last part, but she just didn't hear him. He only said those words to me. When he left, I felt a knot the size of a watermelon swell inside my stomach.

While away, he missed many memory makers. Birthdays, funerals, the Prose goes to preschool party, my first dance recital, our move from the apartment on 3rd Avenue to the bungalows on 10th, and the 2nd Avenue School Father-Daughter Dance.

My uncle escorted me to the dance, which would have been fine if not for the fact that he's only eleven years older than I am and opted for a tuxedo shirt with a bow tie and vest painted on the front instead of spending money to rent a suit.

My granny taught me how to hit a softball. She did a pretty good job, but at my first game, when the pitcher struck me out, she ran out on the field, cursed and kicked the umpire, and then dragged me out of the batter's box. It could have been a clean getaway if not for the fact that her bright-yellow sun hat became wedged in the doorframe of her Chrysler LeBaron. Turning her head from side to side, she crushed the brim of her bonnet as the city view from the baseball diamond orbited around her.

While my father—the astronaut, moonwalker, star cruiser, rocket-riding explorer—was off saving the world, he missed the Prose goes to first grade party, cousin J.C.'s release from juvie, cousin James's first-place win in the science fair, and the emergence of two uninvited guests.

I woke up one day and they were just there. No training bra, no warning sign, just two imposing mounds. I went from sliding head first into home plate and double dutching in double time, to side-sleeping, shoulder-strapping, eyeturning boobs. They were the topic of discussion wherever I went. "What happened?" asked Prose. "Daaaannng!" chimed Derrick, Jamal, and the 2nd

Ave crew. And most irritating was Mercy's: "I'm so proud of you." She said this as if I had purposely set out to produce these oversized objects.

And now at school, Jeanine and Janet are upset because I got 'em first, the boys are cruel because they'll never have 'em, and Mrs. Jensen no longer calls on me even when I raise my hand, which I'm convinced is due to the fact that mine are bigger than hers.

For weeks after my two guests moved in, I went to school, came home, did chores, slept on my side, and started my day all over again. In class I focused on becoming invisible. I willed my existence into the shape of a bird that could fly out the window, out the invisible gates around 2nd Ave, and out of this neighborhood. The brainpower it took to become a bird in flight clouded my hearing, making it impossible for me to recognize the repeated "Miss Hunter. Miss Zora Hunter!" hurtling from Mrs. Jensen's lips. When I opened my eyes, everyone was looking at me. Even Jeanine and Janet had set their eyes in my direction.

"Are we interrupting you, Miss Hunter?"

"No, Mrs. Jensen."

"Are you ready to tell us who you will be bringing to Career Day?"

Career Day. The day when students pretend to care and parents pretend they actually like what they do to pay the light bill.

"Um, for Career Day, I'm going to bring my…father."

"Okay then. It looks like everyone is scheduled."

My father. Even I don't know why I said that. Mercy would never be able to get the time off. My uncle fixes cars with a guy named Titus whose claim to fame is putting five Burger King Whoppers in his mouth at one time. My brain was drained from being a bird. I skipped eating that day. My breasts were expanding by the hour. All these things helped in the creation of one impossible task: bringing my father to Career Day.

When the Friday of Career Day finally arrived, I knew I had to come up with something. That morning, I packed up James's junior scientist mail-order telescope and his poster-size map of the constellations. I would explain to the class, without divulging too much information, the complicated demands of my father's career.

When it was my turn in class, I positioned the telescope on its fold-out legs and held the map in front of me.

"My father sends his deepest regrets for not being able to make it to Career Day. He's an astronaut, so as you can see, it would be very difficult for him to make it here from outer space. I thought he might get a special leave, but he's working on a top-secret mission." I directed that statement at Mrs. Jensen.

"When it's all over, I'm sure he won't mind coming in and showing everyone his space stuff."

I finished my speech and was very proud until the entire class broke into laughter. Their voices chimed together, alternately fading and growing like the school tardy bell. The giggles, high and low, competed with the deep, throaty whispers of parents quieting their kids. I even thought I heard Mrs. Jensen laugh, but I couldn't bear to lower the map, which I now used to hide my tears. I bit down on my lower lip to stop it from quivering, and the louder the laughter, the harder my teeth sunk into my flesh. It was not until I could taste my salty tears mixing with the warm blood in my mouth that I set my unfortunate lip free. Mrs. Jensen motioned me back to my chair, and when I saw the frown on her face and my name written on the board, I knew that I was in trouble.

When the bell rang, Maxine Coleman walked over and said, "My daddy says your daddy is a moonwalker alright. He moonwalked like MJ right out the back door." With that, she rolled her eyes and ran to catch up with her father. I attempted to follow her, but Mrs. Jensen cleared her throat in that don't-you-dare-move type of way. I slumped down deep into my chair.

"Miss Hunter, I admire your creativity, but lying is unacceptable."

"But—"

"No buts. I will have to make a call to your mother."

I wanted to say, Well, that's why mine are bigger than yours. I even opened my mouth to let the words come out. All that exited was "Can I go now?"

"You're dismissed."

As I walked out of the room, I thought I heard her laugh again. My sadness was a huge hand scooping me up and tossing me down the hallway. I was no more than an insignificant pebble skipping across the lake-blue lockers and landing on the school steps. From there, I ran. I ran through the alley and around Pete's liquor store. I ran by To Go's Pizza, and on 4th Ave I ran into Jeanine and Janet. To let me know they were no longer mad, they began to run too. We took all the shortcuts our parents told us not to take. We cut through Mrs. Jackson's backyard and hopped the fence behind the abandoned warehouse. We sprinted across the parking lot of First Zion Baptist Church and darted across Market Street with its broken traffic signal, dodging oncoming traffic, leaving the crossing guard chasing us. We raced all the way to my block and then we stopped. We knew this would be my last stretch of freedom before punishment set in. By this time, the warm air had dried my tears only to make way for fresh ones. Jeanine and Janet reached under their tops and handed me the tissue boobs they had been wearing for the last two weeks.

James was waiting for me when we made it to the house.

"Ain't no use crying now. Your mom got the call and is on her way home from work. I'm s'pose to tell you not to go anywhere. An astronaut, a freakin' astronaut. I always knew you were a space case."

The sky turned purple and then black before Mercy made it home. I spent the time in between watching the headlights of z cars hit my wall and then slide onto the ceiling. I waited for the one that would shine directly into my window to let me know the Toyota had pulled in the driveway. When the waiting dragged endlessly, I closed my eyes as tight as I could and then opened them slowly, allowing the colored circles that appeared before me to bounce off of each other and melt back into blackness. Eventually, I just listened to the ticking of the mahogany clock on the hallway wall. I must have dozed off, because I never saw the headlights or heard the key in the door. It wasn't until she flipped on the light switch that I realized Mercy, and my pending fate, were home.

I jumped out of bed, closed my eyes once more, and dropped my pants. I even flinched twice before I realized I wasn't getting hit.

"Lying is wrong. I've raised you to be an honest person. You must never lie. Even when the truth hurts so much that the lie becomes the only way to lessen the pain, you still mustn't lie."

She yanked up my pants and turned me around to face her. Tears pooled in her eyes. She rubbed the sides of her forehead as if trying to massage away her thoughts. We remained in silence, interrupted only by the theme to *Star Wars,* hummed by James as he walked by my room.

It was one year, nine months, and seventeen days before we saw our father again. He missed the Prose goes to the dentist party, James's graduation from middle school, and the emergence of Jeanine and Janet's four long-awaited guests. He stayed for a week this time. He had a room at the Ramada near school, and every day he stood waiting for me on the same steps where I used to wait for him. He tried going by the house to see Prose, but every time he came, she dove under the dining room table. On the last day, he greeted me with a teddy bear and two giant pixie sticks. Two things I loved when I was nine. The gifts let me know that he was leaving again. It hurt less this time. Only a small knot the size of an acorn rested in my stomach. The taxi pulled up and waited impatiently. My father kissed me on the forehead, twice. Once for me and once for Prose. He had gained weight since the last time, and his poked-out belly pressed painfully against my chest. The cab driver got out and opened the passenger door. My father walked backwards, almost moonwalking, his eyes fixed on me until he bumped into the rear of the cab. As they drove off, I read the bumper sticker on the back of the car: HOLLYWOOD, A PLACE FOR THE STARS. This was to be my Star Cruiser's final landing.

## AUTHOR'S STATEMENT

"Star Cruiser" is from a larger fiction manuscript entitled "The Aves." "The Aves" invites readers to follow young protagonist, Zora Hunter, as she tackles the trials, treasures, and triumphs of girlhood, sisterhood, absentee fatherhood, and the U-shaped borough that is her neighborhood. Through Zora's revelatory accounts, readers meet the colorful characters dwelling in the Aves. The death of an avenue child also serves as a sobering reminder that surviving childhood can be as complex as the intertwined streets of the city of Los Angeles. Growing up, I didn't see literary heroes who looked like me. As a result, I am inspired to create a twist on the hero's journey by crafting characters who breathe life into forgotten civilizations. I am also motivated to unearth the splendor of second chances. Any beauty seen in my characters is my ongoing attempt to resurrect deadened dreams and start again.

The "Star Cruiser" chapter is one of the ways that the theme of second chances appears in the novella. However, as is the case with life, and with death, some chances cannot be recovered. We bear the scars from our own choices and the choices of those who came before us. We also bear the beauty of our strength because scars show our ability to respond to and recover from our wounds.

**RYANE NICOLE GRANADOS** is a Los Angeles native who earned her MFA in creative writing from Antioch University, Los Angeles. Her work has been featured in various publications, including *The Manifest-Station, Forth Magazine, The Nervous Breakdown, Scary Mommy, The Atticus Review,* and *LA Parent Magazine.* She is an alum of Voices of Our Nation Arts Foundation, Bread Loaf Writer's Conference in Sicily, and the Community of Writers at Squaw Valley. Her storytelling has been showcased in the national stage production *Expressing Motherhood* and KPCC's live series *Unheard LA.*

# The Blue Medium

**Lillian Howan**

It is my profession to be lost. When I was an apprentice, my teacher took me to a grove of mape trees, a place where sunlight was hidden, disappearing into the canopy of leaves. The wood of the mape was dark, nearly black, and the trunks opened like wings. "Losing your way is easy," said my teacher.

We had left his pick-up truck by the side of the road and were wandering through the elephant-ear taro that grew in the shadows beneath the mape trees. There arose the scent of things unseen: the earth damp below the thickness of leaves, the smoke from garbage burning far away. Over the ground, the mape spread its roots in serpentine ridges.

The teacher walked to where two roots ran close together, the gap within curving like a narrow boat. "Sit here," he said, and I shook out an empty rice sack and placed it inside. A cloud of mosquitos rose from the ground as I sat. "Are there spirits here?" I asked.

"Sit down and don't move," said the teacher. He was the age of my grandfather and smelled of camphor oil and Hundred Flowers liniment.

I looked up above at the web of branches, the green darkness that obscured the sky. "Will spirits come if I wait?"

"I'll return in the morning," said the teacher walking away towards the road.

I crossed my legs and waited. The air was hot and breathless with the odor of decaying leaves. Mosquitos whined around my ears, and I heard the ocean in the distance, the sound of the waves breaking and receding, the breath of the ocean inhaled and exhaled and inhaled again.

Every day of my apprenticeship, I had sat, motionless for hours inside the teacher's house or outside in his garden of mango trees and tilapia fish ponds. "Look here," said the teacher, pointing to the crack between his doors, double doors, the bottom corner of one broken and partially eaten by termites. "No—you're looking at this side, look here at the center between the doors. Not more to one side or to the other." On the other side of the doors, someone was brooming, sweeping the leaves fallen during the night. "Breathe slowly. Don't be distracted looking this way and that."

I learned to remain still. I learned to focus on the line where the double doors met. I learned to be silent.

"Listen," the teacher always said.

"What am I listening for?" I asked.

"Listen here"—he thumped the center of my chest. "You're just listening with your ears. And what good are those? You won't hear anything." He bent slowly down, and lifting my toes, he pointed at the soles of my feet. "Here is where you listen."

The teacher heard the voices of the spirit world. He would sit in a room other than the one where I sat, the house silent with only the vini vini birds chattering in the trees outside. Nothing would be spoken, and then I would hear him beginning to sing. His song was different from the songs I heard everyday, the san ko, the mountain songs of my great-grandmother or the love songs my aunts sang as they folded the wash. The teacher's song was tuneless, without pattern like an endless thread, his voice twisting, rising, and then disappearing.

When I first started as an apprentice, I was a small boy and I asked the teacher many questions. What did they say? What did they look like? My questions were constant, but the teacher's answer was always the same: listen, be still, listen.

My uncle Freddy, who was only one year older and like a brother, goaded me at home with gruesome tales of tupapaus, the spirits of the dead. "They'll catch you and eat you alive," he said. He told me that a boy in Bora Bora had been captured by a sorcerer and many days later part of his head was found under his family's doorstep. "Crabs were crawling out of his skull," said Freddy, "and his eyes were eaten away."

I recounted this to the teacher and he laughed. "Is it true?" I asked.

"Maybe you should go home and not return anymore," he replied still laughing.

"Is it true?"

"Go sit by the doors," he said. "Maybe a ghost will appear and explain these things to you."

I sat and sat. Every day I listened and the years of my apprenticeship accumulated waiting for the spirit voices to sing for me.

I sat, the hours passing, and the end of the day approached. The branches of the mape curved above and veils of light fell through the leaves when the wind was still. I tried to think of my breath flowing in and out, and then I was thinking about dinner.

The nut of the mape tree was kidney-shaped and enclosed in a wooden shell. Along the road to Papeete, street vendors sold mapes boiled and strung on niau, the thin sticks running through the centers of palm leaves. Grandfather sometimes bought mapes, and then the younger cousins danced about, their hands outstretched, shouting "ma-pay! ma-pay!"—the mapes as large as the palm of their hands. The nut always bore a knife-mark, a cut on the corners and along the flesh where the machete blade had split the shell.

I thought of mapes fallen among the leaves waiting to be gathered. The taste was mild and sweet, and I had all night to sit still, waiting for spirits to appear. I had never seen a spirit, but I had eaten mapes and before the evening light faded, I thought my time better spent searching for something I knew I could find.

The earth was wet and sank like a sponge. I walked over tree roots, twisting along the ground, and the empty hulls of mapes. At home my cousins, Freddy, and my aunts, my grandparents, and parents would be eating dinner: bean curd, dried shrimp, peppers stuffed with finely-ground fish, chicken and black mushrooms. I continued walking—perhaps there were mapes fallen in the shade of the next tree, behind a branch, among the roots.

The sunset light dimmed, and the shadows spread quickly. I turned back, the black trunks of the trees looming, suddenly unfamiliar and unrecognizable, a pattern of vines and leaves dissolving into the unbroken shadow of the night. Where had the teacher asked me to sit? Behind this shadowy ridge of roots? Beyond this field of taro? I had found nothing, not a single nut. There was only the soft, sucking mud beneath my feet and darkness all around. The night descended, and I did not know where I was.

The wind rose, erasing the sound of the ocean. A rooster crowed and a dog began barking. The barking seemed far away, muffled by the dense surrounding trees. It would be a long walk to the nearest house, guided by the glimmer of distant sounds.

Above in the treetops, a seabird awakened and called, a rasping, creaking sound. A piece of skull, Freddy had said, the crabs had swallowed the eyes. I sat down at the foot of a mape, my back against the trunk, and waited. A ghost was detected by its perfume, I had heard—a scent like frangipani. Along the road that passed before the house where my family lived, trees of frangipani bloomed, the flowers pink and yellow, red and the colors of sunset. The scent crept at night through the open windows over our beds where we slept enveloped in mosquito netting.

My grandfather had once seen a ghost. He told me this story often, talking as he closed the locks to his store near the waterfront of Papeete. He had been bicycling from the town where he played mahjong at night. The road had been empty, his dog following behind as he pedaled along the hedges of hibiscus and crotons. As he turned past the flamboyant trees, he saw someone crossing the road, a woman dressed in white. She was wearing a white hat as if it were Sunday morning and she was on her way to church, but it was night and all the churches were closed. Grandfather slowed his pedaling as the woman walked towards the middle of the road, but his dog ran ahead barking. The woman turned, and Grandfather saw that she held a cluster of grapes in her hand, her face hidden beneath her hat.

Grapes did not grow where we lived, on the island of Tahiti; they were imported and they were rare. Grandfather said these grapes were purple, almost red, shining in the moonlight beneath the woman's hand. Even Fwi-lin his dog stopped barking and paused, whining and sniffing the air. Grandfather swung one leg from his bicycle. The woman stretched out her arm dangling the grapes, and for a moment, Grandfather saw her face—the face of a young girl no older than ten or eleven. She was so young, a child in a woman's dress, that Grandfather shouted in surprise, and then she vanished. Fwi-lin barked and snapped at the air, but there was nothing in the road—no girl, no grapes—only Grandfather alone with his bicycle.

I had tasted grapes once when I was fifteen. I had accompanied Grandfather and Father to a dinner at the house of Monsieur Lesage. Grandfather introduced me, his eldest grandson, and there was polite talk about my interest in languages and the possibility of my being sent to the University of Paris. We were Hakka and, according to Father, the Hakka had a gift for languages. He said this whenever we visited the house of someone French. I never paid attention; I always heard this story—my father explaining that in China we were called the guest people and how for a thousand years we had wandered, across China and Southern Asia, among a multitude of dialects and that we learned to translate one object into many names.

Monsieur Lesage sat in a wicker chair beneath a painting of coconut palms, the colors washed in dark green, purple, and yellow light. He owned two freighters, the Mareva and the Moana Nui, and transported cargo from the South China Sea to Papeete. He said he had lived in Saigon many years ago and there he heard that the Hakka were the most fanatical, the most secretive; they had lost one of the bloodiest civil wars in history and were said to possess a secret so that they did not fear death.

This was nonsense, Father replied. People always told exotic stories, but in the end everyone was afraid of death. When a war was lost, many died regardless of whether they were afraid or not.

"They died or they came to Tahiti," said Grandfather, and he and Monsieur

Lesage laughed. They were both large men and everything about them seemed rectangular and solid—their faces, their backs, their hands. Around us the furniture bore a smooth sheen, chairs and shelves covered with a dustless glow.

We ate beef bourguignon and potatoes dauphinoise in the dining room overlooking the sea, the ceiling fans above turning slowly. At the end of dinner, a plate of cheese accompanied by a bowl of fruit was brought to the table. The fruit was not local, but imported by air—apples, grapes, plums and mirabelles. The fruit was refrigerated, a fine layer of condensation already covering the cold skin. I selected an apple and a plum and picked up my knife. The image of my mother appeared briefly, shaking her head no. "Jonathan why two? And such a large plum," she said. "One is enough."

I glanced at Grandfather—he was puffing on a cigar, the tip turning from ash to incandescent as he inhaled. Father was talking, heatedly discussing the Assembly elections, his head bent sideways towards Monsieur Lesage. I reached across the table and plucked a small cluster of grapes. I ate the plum, scooping the red flesh with a spoon, and then I ate the grapes, peeling them one by one. The grapes were yellow-green and the seeds were large and tear-shaped. The apple I ate last, slicing it open with a knife, the red vein around the seed-core curved like a heart.

I thought of apples, red grapes, mapes and beef bourguignon, chicken with black mushrooms—all the food I was not eating and the dinner I had missed. The night stretched endlessly, each moment passing, slow as an hour. I closed my eyes, I opened my eyes, the darkness remained unchanged.

When I first became an apprentice, I imagined myself calling forth different spirits every night, my uncle Freddy and my cousins at my mercy. I saw them fetching the sweetest mangos for me and doing all my homework. No longer would I do the usual chores, feeding the chickens and the pigs, awakening early—Freddy was always still asleep—to bring the bread for breakfast in the morning.

My dreams of glory vanished though when I discovered the nature of my apprenticeship. It was monotonous, long, and relentlessly unremarkable. I had been an apprentice for seven years, and I was sixteen—seventeen in November—and what had I learned? Nothing. No magic formulas, no incantations. No spirits appeared when I called. Except for my parents, most of my family had forgotten I was an apprentice—I remained so ordinary. Every afternoon after school, I walked to the house of the teacher, an old wooden house surrounded by hedges of ginger. Every evening, I returned home late, to eat the dinner my mother had set aside for me alone, before starting my homework for school.

I knew only how to sit and how to listen, and I was listening for nothing. I heard only silence.

In the night, the wood of the mapes creaked, settling into the earth and there was the rainlike patter of lizards running through the leaves. Dampness clung to my skin and the seabirds called, the same repeated rasping call. I thought it impossible to sit longer.

I shifted my weight, trying to remember the direction where the road lay, but before I could stand, there was a noise. My eyes opened. The darkness was moving—a rustle, a faint creaking. Something approached beneath the trees.

I stared into the tangle of branches, but there were only shadows and I saw nothing. The rustling paused, and I could feel it searching the air. I felt the dryness in my throat. I stayed very still. Was it an animal, a man? A tupapau? It had not found me yet. It was still looking through the darkness where I sat.

The leaves shuffled; it was moving again, coming closer. I turned my eyes away and then I heard the voice of the teacher. I saw him, the way he always bent, frowning towards me. "Your breath goes in and out," he would say. Look here at the center. It is easy to be lost.

My head was heavy, as if something were pressing from above. I closed my eyes. "Don't be distracted," the teacher said. Don't look this way and that.

I took in my breath, and in the next moment, I felt a sudden quiet. All my senses had been straining, looking outside—at the trees where the unknown was moving, towards the darkness where the road might be. But then I felt the roots beneath my legs and beneath my feet. I felt the trunk along my back. I felt the absolute stillness. Above, the tree branches bent and waved in the wind, below the roots creaked within the earth, but in the center of the tree where I sat, nothing moved and it was silent.

The shadows approached and I felt a sudden weight upon my head, but they were distant and I was far removed. I was enclosed in stillness. I was lost, and in the silence, I disappeared.

The teacher was tapping my shoulder. My neck felt sore; I had fallen asleep. I opened my eyes. It was early dawn, the grove suffused with a faint grey light. The branches and leaves had turned silver and the air was like mist. I was still sitting.

The teacher looked at me gravely.

I tried to speak, but my voice was cracked and dry. "I saw nothing," I said. "I heard nothing."

He nodded his head. "Good."

"I did not sing," I said.

He smiled. "No, you were snoring."

"Will the dead sing through my voice?" I asked.

The teacher bent over me, lifting something from the top of my head. The heaviness cleared, and I saw what it was: the nut seed of the mape, without shell, perfectly smooth and unmarked. He put it in my hand. The seed was light. In my hand, it weighed hardly at all.

---

**AUTHOR'S STATEMENT**

When I was a child, my mother told me stories about her family name. Pronounced Mu in the Hakka dialect that my parents spoke, this name means a shaman or a sorcerer. My mother had a strict sense of the truth and did not tolerate exaggeration, but I loved elaborating and embellishing the truth. My mother's stories about her Mu name fascinated me, but she was stern about not encouraging my predilection for the dramatic.

My mother was born on the island of Raiatea, where she lived with her grandparents. She told me that she had a great-uncle who was so tall that he could pluck a bird from a tree. He went to buy bread for the family early in the morning, and sometimes when he returned, he amused my mother by showing her a wild bird that he released from his hand, allowing it to fly free back into the trees. As a boy, he was trained by his teacher in the Mu village in China. The teacher taught the young boys of the village, but only one would become his true apprentice.

"What would happen to the other boys?" I asked.

My mother explained that they would learn martial arts and would grow up to farm or to sell things.

"What would happen to the apprentice?" I asked.

"He learned to put himself in a trance," said my mother. She spoke of such things subtly and indirectly. She believed that truth was complicated, multi-layered, and that words were signposts pointing in the direction of something complex and vast, beyond simple explanations.

My mother passed away in Hawai'i when I was in my twenties, and in the years after her passing, certain images would appear and reappear in my dreams: perfume bottles, birds, and their songs. Like the scent of perfume or a melody that repeats itself in one's memory, the images lingered, and I found myself dwelling on their enigma. Gradually, I began to write down words—an image, a phrase, sentence by sentence—the words seeming to grow as if the dream images were the seeds, and from these dream seeds, my stories developed, taking root in the memories of my mother's stories.

**LILLIAN HOWAN** spent her early childhood in Tahiti and later graduated from the University of California, Berkeley, School of Law. Her writings have been published in *Asian American Literary Review, Café Irreal, Calyx, Jellyfish Review, New England Review, South Dakota Review, Vice-Versa,* and the anthology *Under Western Eyes.* She is the editor of *Rosebud and Other Stories,* a collection by legendary playwright Wakako Yamauchi. Her debut novel *The Charm Buyers* received the Ka Palapala Poʻokela Award for Excellence.

# Two Poems

**Gerda Govine Ituarte**

### VISIT TO GODFATHER'S

Sunday afternoons,
Dad visits Godfather.
        Seven years old,
        get to go!

Eyes on the move.
Fat, thin books line carved wood bookcases.
Magazines capture corners of glass table.
Easels hold watercolor flowers—
flamboyant, orange, yellow, red hibiscus
vie for attention.

Unfazed by my lap hopping,
living room mentor,
well-dressed young men talk serious stuff.
Questions rise.
        Answers land
amidst wrinkled brows,
smiles, joke or two.

Delicious aroma saturates air!
Slip into garden,
spy white table,
rainbow-colored straw mats,
chicken, stew, rice and peas,
fried plantains,

Johnnycake,
papaya and mango juice,
pineapple, coconut, guava tarts.
Motion to Godfather,
Time to eat!

All rise,
disappear one by one,
wash hands,
fill chairs in waiting.
Food blessed.
Leaders nourished.
Renaissance blooms!

## BOY CHILD*

*I'd be crawling on all fours to get to you*
*I didn't realize his loudest cry for help was silence*

Boy child quiet
Boy did not bother anyone

Boy child slow
Boy child withdrawal peaked at fourteen

Boy child scared to talk on phone
Boy child wanted to be a neuroscientist

Boy child isolated
Boy child attended college

Boy child never hurt anyone
Boy child communicated by email

Boy child visits home slowed down
Boy child disappeared

Boy child bought guns
Boy child stockpiled body armor

Boy child mass murdered
Boy child, my own son

Boy child what could I have done differently?

**Maria L. La Ganga, "James Holmes through mother's tearful eyes,"* Los Angeles Times, *July 30, 2015.*

---

**GERDA GOVINE ITUARTE** is the author of four poetry collections: *Poetry Within Reach in Unexpected Places* (2018), *Future Awakes in Mouth of NOW* (2016), *Alterations/Thread Light Through Eye of Storm* (2015), and *Oh, Where is My Candle Hat?* (2012). She established the Pasadena Rose Poets in 2016. In February 2017 she instituted poetry reading at Pasadena city council meetings. She is the editor of *Pasadena Rose Poets Poetry Collection 2019: Reflection. Resistance. Reckoning. Resurrection* (Shabda Press, Pasadena, California). Her poetry has been featured in exhibits at Art Produce, Avenue 50 Studio, California Center for the Arts Museum, El Gatito Gallery, New Americans Museum, The Front Gallery, and Vromans. Her work is included in the *Altadena Poetry Review, Coiled Serpent, Dryland Arts and Letters, Journal of Modern Poetry, Ms. Aligned,* and *Spectrum.* Selected readings include Avenue 50 Studio, Beyond Baroque, Huntington Gardens, LitFest Pasadena, Pasadena Museum of Contemporary Art, The Last Bookstore, and The World Stage. She resides with Luis Ituarte, her artist husband, at El Rancho Alegre (Artist Dreamland) in Jamul, California.

She has curated two international art exhibits at Avenue 50 Studio. The KPBS Audio Podcast "Only Here" featured *Dia de los Muertos,* her and her husband's project journey from Baja, California, to the 2018 California Center for the Arts Escondido Museum Exhibit "Des Escondido No Longer Hidden."

"Boy Child" is reprinted from *Future Awakes in Mouth of NOW* (Éditions du Cygne [SWAN World], Paris, France: 2016). "Visit to Godfather's" is reprinted from *Oh, Where is My Candle Hat?* (Asterico Editora de Poesia, Tijuana, B.C., Mexico: 2012).

# The Prince of Mournful Thoughts

**Caroline Kim**

Last week, a fragment of a long document from the 18th century thought to be written to a foreigner was unearthed at a private property undergoing renovation in Cheongdam. The writer's name is unknown but he is believed to be a royal secretary in the court of King Yongjo, Korea's most beloved king.

*Seoul Shinmun*, February 12, 2018

Around this time, Prince Sado's obsession with clothes began. In order to impress the King, Prince Sado began to take great care with his clothes, buying up all the silks that arrived from China so that there was hardly any left over for others. He ordered upwards of thirty sets of new clothes at a time, burning some as an offering to the spirit gods. He had to try on many different robes before selecting one, discarding them because they were too long, too short, too plain, too bright, too tight, too loose, too scratchy, too unlucky. He changed so often, his skin became raw and overly sensitive. Sometimes he bled from the skin. Once he was dressed, he would wear the same suit of clothes for days until they became rank and filthy. In this way, everybody, except the King, came to know about the Prince's illness.

It became an especial problem for Lord Hong, the Prince's father-in-law. Since the Prince's allowance was insufficient to his need for the best silks, Lord Hong sold some of his own best agricultural lands in the South to pay for it. Both Prince Sado and his daughter, Lady Hong, could be put in great jeopardy if the King discovered the Prince's actions. The King wouldn't see the Prince's pathetic appeal to him, he would only see the foolishness of wasting money on silks, and indeed of the mind that was so narrowly obsessed with clothes. It would prove once again how disappointing was his son, how little fit to be King.

But much could be hidden from the King. Because he did not like his son, he preferred trying to forget him.

---

This story is a fictional account of an historical event. Crown Prince Sado lived between 1735 and 1762.

The Prince had a roomful of seamstresses working day and night making ceremonial robes to wear in the King's presence. One of these seamstresses was a palace maid named Sunbi whom he first saw at his mother's residence. For us who worked in the Prince's palace, she was at first truly heaven sent.

Sunbi was a fair-faced girl of sixteen, fresh from the provinces, a little chubby, a little simple. The Prince took to visiting his mother more often, arranging to meet Sunbi afterward. Without anybody noticing, he managed to get her a job hemming and ironing for his seamstresses. Like a true peasant, she worshipped Prince Sado, and loved Lady Hong. She never worried Lady Hong might feel jealous of her; in her mind, it was unthinkable that the Prince could love her more than he loved Lady Hong. After all, she was a slave.

But the Prince did love her. He respected, but could not love, his wife. Lady Hong was everything he was not—filial, obedient, graceful in her duties. She was never late for the early morning greetings required by tradition to the King, the Queen, and the Dowager Mother, all at their different residences. She did not seize up when asked a question by the King, but answered clearly and succinctly, and in a manner that even caused the King to smile. Prince Sado could never manage this. Worst of all, Lady Hong was even loving towards him, calming him when he was distraught, sending him healing teas and medicines, and giving him good advice about how to behave in the King's presence.

With Sunbi, it was he, the Prince, who gave freely, openly, presenting her with gifts of jewelry and cloth that amazed her, awed her. He loved her simpleness, how she asked for nothing but delighted in everything. He liked watching her eat, sleep, laugh. He understood something new when he was with her, something he imagined most peasants must already know: that taking care of the woman you loved, generously, gracefully, was the pinnacle of human happiness. His usually anxious mind was calmed when he was with Sunbi. He could imagine having been born into another life outside of court.

For a time, the Prince righted himself. He gave up his strange reading, stopped wandering at night, only changed his clothes once or twice a day. He returned to his duties. His mother, Lady Sonhui, rejoiced and even the King began to hear good things about the Prince. For the first time, the King invited Prince Sado on the annual visit to the hot baths in Kaesong.

The Prince was overjoyed. He had never been invited to Kaesong by the King, nor anywhere, despite being Prince Regent, though the Princesses often went along. Thus, he had never experienced for himself the festive air of the King's train and how the people lined up on either side of the road and waved their handkerchiefs and shouted, "Long Live Your Majesty!"

However, on the day they set off, a hard rain began to fall, not stopping for even a minute, drenching the entire retinue and making everyone miserable.

Even the crowds, who normally rushed the roads, stayed away, causing the King's mood to deteriorate. Halfway to Kaesong, King Yongjo called a halt to the procession and demanded that the Prince be sent back to the Palace. He blamed Prince Sado for the inclement weather, saying every other time he had gone, the weather had been pleasant and warm. The Prince was understandably distraught. "There is no way I can go on living now," he said.

Upon returning to the Palace, the Prince consulted with his regular shamans who read his face and his hands, tossed grains of sand. They told him what he feared and longed for most—the throne, and his father's love. They only made his mind more unsteady, and when the King returned a few days later, chastened by the Dowager Queen for his thoughtless and superstitious actions against the Prince, he found the Prince's private quarters in disarray, the Prince himself bewildered of mind and body. King Yongjo even thought he smelled wine in his rooms even though it is strictly forbidden in the Palace. This was not the case, not yet, but the King was so angry, he slapped the Prince harshly across the face and declared that he would never be allowed outside the Palace again.

You may be wondering why this King and Prince were always at odds with each other. It started from the very beginning.

The Prince was a solemn child, slight of build, long-necked, with a sad expression in his eyes. Perhaps this was because he was always lonely, having been taken from his mother when he was only 100 days old and moved to the Prince Regent's palace. Privately, we all thought this separation too early but the King had been waiting anxiously for an heir, ever since his first son, Prince Hyojong, died many years earlier. By the time Prince Sado was born, the King had already been on the throne for twenty-five years and complained often of the heavy burden he carried. Thus, he wished to establish Prince Sado independently from the beginning.

During his early years, the Prince's mother, Lady Sonhui, came often, sometimes daily, and was even sometimes accompanied by the King, but it was not the same as living under the same roof with one's own parents, and the Crown Prince learned early on that everyone he loved would go away after a time. Until the Prince married at the age of ten, there were no children around him. He sometimes visited with his sisters, the Princesses Hwasun, Hwapyong, and Hwahyop but not very often. And when they did, they sat in a room like grown-ups—conversing while eating sweets and drinking tea.

Most of the time, Prince Sado was surrounded by silly court ladies and lazy eunuchs who let him do whatever he pleased.

According to those who knew of the Prince's early years, he was an extremely bright child who delighted and astonished his parents by walking at four months and speaking at six months. At seven months, he could point to the four cardinal directions. At three, he could recite half of Confucius's Analects. But at five, he suffered an ailment of unknown origin. It struck suddenly, taking all strength from him, and for many months, the palace feared they might lose him. But he recovered, though he was pale and listless for many months, and some say he was much changed by his illness.

In terms of temperament, the Prince was a thoughtful child, slow to make decisions, listening carefully to others without letting his own opinion be known. In this way, he was quite different from the King who was extremely decisive and opinionated. Where the one acted quickly, the other hesitated, unsure which path to take. One could see from the beginning how unfortunate it was that Prince Sado and King Yongjo had such different personalities. The King simply could not understand why it took the Prince so long to answer a question by the Royal Tutors, and he made his frustrations plain, shouting at the Prince to answer more quickly. He mistakenly took the Prince's silence as a sign of stubbornness. As a result, he demanded the Prince spend even more time studying with the Royal Tutors. He even grew so angry he stopped inviting the Prince to royal banquets and celebrations unless it would seem odd if he was not present.

All the Prince wanted to do was please the King, but he did not know how. When the King posed a question such as: In times of uncertainty in a Kingdom, when the people are suffering from drought and pestilence, should a ruler follow the ways of T'ang in the first century or Chu Kow in the 14th? Well, the Prince thought, one could be like T'ang, who believed a ruler should open up his coffers and share the fate of his people or like Chu Kow who thought the ruler must be protected, first and foremost, in order that he could live to serve his people. The Prince could always see two sides to every question. How could he choose? And yet, the Prince was also keenly aware that his father was expecting a wise answer. He started to speak T'ang's name, then stopped. He began to say Chu Kow—but hesitated. The King would then berate the prince in front of all the ministers in the main audience hall.

The Prince began to dread the morning audiences, and who could blame him? Half the time, the King ignored his presence, not once looking in his direction. Or if he did notice him he grumbled about his clothing, his hair or his tardiness. There was some justification for this. For when the Prince became terrified of the King, he began acting in such a way that could only bring more scorn down upon him. For example, so anxious was he about meeting his father that he would wake in the dark, even before the bells from the water tower rang to lift the nightly curfew, and demand to be dressed in his royal robes. Then he would sit at his desk before a lighted lamp and commence memorizing his books, until inevitably, he fell asleep again. He would snarl at the eunuchs who came to wake him, and though they nudged and pushed without seeming to, he was late washing his face, and combing his hair. His clothes by this time were, of course, rumpled and untidy. Without fail, the Prince found himself morning after morning, running to the main audience hall in Changdok Palace, his mind so filled with useless information he could hardly remember his own name. Of course, all this further infuriated the King.

As if this weren't bad enough, he then became afflicted with a terrible stutter that only appeared in the King's presence. When the King heard the Prince's stutter, he grew enraged and made fun of him in the company of others. The Prince paled and cowered before him. The very sight of the Prince grew to disgust the King.

We, who lived in the Prince's palace, loved and feared for the Prince. We saw how he struggled to gain the King's favor, and how he suffered under his father's disappointed glare. It was sad for all concerned.

After the Prince was forbidden from leaving the palace, we who lived with him could see the Prince had given up. He stopped trying to please the King altogether. He gave himself fully over to his own desires, playing more and more war games with the Royal Guards, and even disguising himself and leaving the Palace to wander about the capital, consorting with prostitutes and unscrupulous men. He invited them to his residence, holding parties that lasted several days and nights, examples of debauchery that is still sickening to remember. But even that was not enough. Now he was truly turned and could find only one way to relieve his burdens.

The first time it was an accident. He was sword-fighting with a royal soldier attached to guard him, a man whom he respected and who had taught him many maneuvers. They had been fighting for an hour in the full sun when the soldier, an older man, began to tire. He tripped on the root of a tree and as he fell, his sword tipped up and grazed the Prince's arm, drawing a thin line of blood. At first the Prince laughed, then an evil look crossed his face and he fell upon the man and severed his neck. Everyone was quite shocked. Most of all, the Prince. He recoiled and threw his sword aside. Then he turned and ran back to the palace. He tore off his clothes and demanded they be burned. We gathered up the soldier's body and took it outside the Palace. Nobody spoke of it again, and the soldier's family was too fearful to complain. We knew that some terrible line had been crossed, and once crossed, the way back could not be found. The air grew heavy.

But some months passed with no further incident and we told ourselves that it was just an accident and that the Prince had reacted without thinking.

Then one day, when he had put on and taken off twenty different robes, finally wearing only his underclothes, he asked for great quantities of wine to be brought to him. For ever since the King accused him of bringing wine into the Palace, the Prince had begun to do so.

That night, a shaman who was drunk told the Prince that his life would end in a horrible manner, by suffocation. In a different mood, the Prince might have laughed it off, spared the man. But it had been a particularly bad day. The King had once again reduced the Prince's household budget. So when the shaman spoke his thoughtless words, the Prince flared up with rage, and called the shaman a fraud. Having realized his foolishly, deadly error, the now sober man kneeled before the Prince, apologizing, rubbing his hands together, begging forgiveness. But the Prince pulled his favorite dagger out of his clothes and stabbed him in the stomach. Because it did not kill him straightaway, the Prince stabbed the man many more times before pushing the bleeding body away from him.

There were perhaps ten people in the room, all of us frozen and helpless. Finally, Eunuch Han stepped forward and in a calm voice said, "Perhaps the Prince would like his nightly bath," while the Prince nodded and wiped the blade of his dagger on the dead man's robe. He said, "I feel better now that he is dead. I feel an enormous sense of relief!" We tried not to show our horror.

One morning after the King imitated the Prince stuttering at a morning audience with the ministers, the Prince came home shouting for his horse. He played war all that afternoon with several dozen of his royal guard, drawing blood and bruising without seriously hurting anyone. He began drinking as soon as he went back indoors, sitting in his private chamber, alone with his mournful thoughts. By the time a eunuch appeared with his nightly snack of ddukboki and red bean cakes, he was pacing the room and talking aloud. He had opened a chest of weapons he kept in his room, was fingering the inlaid pearl on his favorite sword, testing the curved tip of the blade.

Without looking up, he told the eunuch he would count to ten and then he would chase him down like a boar in the woods. "Excuse me, your Majesty?" said the eunuch, lifting his head in surprise.

"Run!" the Prince shouted.

But the poor eunuch remained standing there, unsure what to do, and was taken completely by surprise when the Prince threw his dagger at him, hitting him in the upper arm. The eunuch shouted and grabbed the offended limb, blood dampening his fingers. Without thinking any more about the matter, he turned and ran away. He fled to the courtyard, the Prince whooping behind him, shouting at his guards to step aside. He had a spear in his hand and chased the eunuch through his gardens, finally catching him near the back wall. He took his time, running him back and forth like a rabbit, before he finally ran toward the eunuch, screaming, his spear raised high. He stabbed him in the abdomen. Then, looking completely crazed, he took out a knife and hacked at the eunuch's neck until it was separated from his body. He stuck it on his spear and raised it high.

From this moment forward, none of us could be at peace. We were all besieged by fear, not knowing when we might be killed. None were safe—royal physicians, court ladies, eunuchs, palace workmen, translators, musicians, shamans—every day several bodies were carried out of the Prince's palace. Eventually, even the King could no longer ignore the horrors taking place and had an audience with the Prince.

"Why are you killing people?" the King asked.

The Prince bowed his head and replied, "It gives me relief."

"Relief! From what?"

"From shame, your Majesty."

"Why do you feel shame?"

"Because you do not love me, your Majesty, and because I am a constant disappointment to you." The Prince then confessed the exact number of people he had killed, and even provided details on how he had done so. We who were present expected the King to be fearfully angry and perhaps even strike the Prince with his own hands, but instead, he was quiet before saying, "I understand. I will try to act differently in the future, if you will."

The Prince was very surprised and tears coursed down his face. "Thank you, your Heavenly Grace. I will not act this way again."

How wonderful and unexpected! I slept well that night for the first night in many months.

For a time after the Prince's audience with the King, we were hopeful that the Prince would right himself. However, it was too late. Whatever this sickness was, it had taken too tight a hold on the Prince's mind. One morning, Sunbi was helping him dress as he had killed the eunuch tasked with dressing him. His skin was red and hot to the touch. Born under an unlucky moon, she scratched him with her nail as she was helping his arm into his sleeve, and enraged, he began to beat her. He must have forgotten who she was, the mother of his two youngest children, and the only person he had ever felt at peace with. Though we could hear her scream terribly, we could do nothing to save her, so we wrung our hands and trembled, beating our chests in frustration and fear, praying it would not end with her death. When the Prince was exhausted and numb, he stumbled out in his bloodied clothing and calling for his horse, went riding off Buddha knows where.

We ran in to where Sunbi was laying on the ground, insensible, though her labored breathing let us know she was still alive. Her face was unrecognizable, soft and misshapen, her nose and cheekbones broken, her jaw out of alignment, her eyes like grapefruits, sealed shut with blood. We called the royal physicians and had her moved to Lady Hong's residence where we hoped she could stay hidden until she healed. But alas, her injuries were too severe and there was not much the royal physicians could do for her. By the evening of the same day, she passed.

Poor girl! How unfortunate she was to catch the eye of the Prince! She had loved him purely and sincerely; if only her love could have given the Prince what the King could not. I will never forget the sight of her poor children crying piteously before they were sent out of the Palace for their protection. Lord Hong gave Sunbi's family a great deal of money for funeral expenses so that they were able to swallow their resentment.

When the Prince returned to his residence and learned what had happened to Sunbi, he made no change in his expression and never spoke her name again.

A few days later, the Prince slept for an unusually long time. The ladies who attended him could not rouse him with loud clapping or movements around his body. Of course, no one dared touch him. We could see he still took breath, but it was shallow and uneven. Finally, a eunuch was dispatched to bring a physician.

The man was trembling even before he entered the Prince's quarters, and started shaking visibly as he grew close to the Prince's form. Clumsily, he opened his medical box, filled with small glass bottles and powders wrapped in specially waxed paper. He pulled out a vial and held his hand over the stopper, ready to remove it, but froze. "I cannot," he said. "I am afraid."

I grew impatient with this cowardly man, and took the vial from him. "What do I do with it?" I asked.

"Hold it under his nose, just briefly," he said. "And the Prince should wake."

I did as he told me. The Prince jerked once, turned his head away and then back, before opening his eyes. They were glazed and unfocused.

"Good morning, your Majesty," I said as cheerfully as I could while pressing back the fear everybody felt in that moment. "How do you feel?"

"How do you expect me to feel waking up with the lot of you staring into my face. Out! Out!" He shooed everyone out except myself and the ladies assigned to help him relieve himself.

"How are you feeling?" I asked again, keeping my head bowed low so nothing could upset him.

"How do you expect me to feel when the Palace is against me?" he asked.

"I do not think the Palace is against you," I said timidly. "There are many here who love you and want only the best for you."

He snorted, taking off all his clothes, holding onto his manhood, while the ladies tried mightily to avert their eyes. I might have laughed in another situation.

"How would you know anything?" he said. "You don't know what it's like to be the son of the King. You don't know what it is to be hated and scorned by your own father."

"If I may, your Majesty, the King wants you to be at peace."

The Prince stormed up close to me, grabbed my face in both his hands and stared at me directly in the eyes. They glittered with a terrifying menace and he smiled in a way that made my body go cold and blank. It took the greatest effort of my life not to quiver but I knew without a doubt that if I did, he would kill me.

"You dare to tell me what the King thinks? What the King wants? You presume to know more about him than I do?"

Never breaking off his staring, he reached down for the dagger he kept always in his robes, then realized he was naked. For a second, uncertainty loomed large. Suddenly, he pushed me away and laughed. "Fool," he said. "You know nothing."

Catching myself before I fell down, I righted myself and bent over at the waist, bowing and saying, "I know nothing. I know nothing."

Once out of the room, I held my chest trying to hold down the galloping legs of my heart. I wanted to run out of the Palace, but caught in misfortune after misfortune, I could not.

In one of his lucid conversations with Lady Hong, Prince Sado terrified her by saying about their son, "Now that the King has a grandson with whom he feels great affinity, he no longer needs me and will kill me off soon. When that happens, please remember me fondly."

Indeed, it was true that young Prince Chongjo was a great favorite of his grandfather's. A bright, confident child, he shared many traits with the King. When he was only seven, the King invested him as a Royal Grandson, and a little later on, as Grand Heir. Even though a child, he was invited by the King to attend the Morning Audience of the Ministers where the King's many praises were recorded by the court annalist. "The Royal Grandson is smart and dutiful," it was written the King said. "I will entrust my kingdom to him."

Now, the Crown Prince loved his son and was never less than kind to him when they were together, exhibiting no signs of jealousy or anger. However, since he did not have a natural father-son relationship with his own father, how could he be expected to know how to behave with his son?

Knowing that his son was greatly favored by the King, Prince Sado asked the court annalist to send him the speeches that were made in the Morning Audiences. When he read how the King extolled the many virtues of the Royal Grandson, his face would turn red and he would shout for wine to be brought to him. "He loves and praises the Royal Grandson," the Prince would say, "when he never showed any affection for me. Why? Why?" It was a certainty on those days that one or more would be killed.

Lady Hong rightly grew fearful that the Prince might attack his son if he continued thinking in this manner and entreated her father to have those passages cut out of the court recordings. Everyone participated in keeping hidden the King's true feelings toward his grandson so that Prince Chongjo would be kept safe. What a situation this was! Between these three generations there was only strife and misunderstandings. Indeed it was most tragic for Prince Chongjo who truly loved his father and grandfather, and wished for them to be at peace. Alas, it was impossible.

Now, the Prince became obsessed with death. He turned his rooms into a tomb, even constructing a bier that he slept in. Once that was complete, he began excavating a great underground tunnel that would lead from his residence to the others. Rooms were created underground, big enough to house all his weapons and even horses, should the need arise. He began threatening other royal family members, saying he would come through the tunnels and kill them in their beds. The whole court was in disarray.

By March, life had become so unbearable in the Palace that the Minister of the Right committed suicide. Within the next two weeks, the Minister of the Left and the new Minister of the Right also killed themselves. Lady Hong tried to hurt herself but was stopped before she could injure herself critically. I vowed to leave the Palace but could find no way of doing so. The Prince had always left us royal secretaries unmolested as he was afraid of what would be written down for future ages, but now nothing seemed certain, and we all wished and prayed to be relieved of our duties. Of course, there was no one who wanted to take our place.

Finally, the brother of a workman who had been killed sent a memorial to the King asking for justice. At first, the King turned his anger on the man who sent the memorial and had him killed for his insolence. Then, upset and confused, he went to Lady Sonhui and asked her what should be done.

This kind lady who had suffered so much already assured the King she would visit the Prince and see if he could be helped. She knew it was hopeless but blamed the sickness and not her son. When she arrived at the Prince's residence, she came upon a strange scene.

Prince Sado had prepared an elaborate feast for her as though it was an important royal occasion. He had tables piled high with fruit and even served ginseng cake and wine. The Prince read aloud a poem he had written on long life. Further, he arranged a big parade in her honor, so that while they ate, Royal Guards in new, brightly colored clothing rode by waving their banners while a military band played behind them. There were dancers and many musicians playing *gayageum,* a long stringed instrument with a sorrowful sound. Then a palanquin appeared with a flag raised high above it, accompanied by trumpets blaring and drums beating. Lady Sonhui was surprised when she was asked to ride in it, for it was most inappropriate. But she was so frightened by this exhibition of the Prince's madness that she dutifully got in and was carried around the Prince's residence. Though she was supposed to spend the night, she excused herself by saying she was not feeling well and went away. Before she did so, she took Lady Hong aside and gripping her hands tightly, said, "What should we do? How are we to act? It seems so hopeless." The two women wept together.

Returning to her own residence, she dictated a letter to the King which read:

> A mother should never write these words and yet I am left with no other recourse. In order to protect the life of the Royal Grandson and to preserve intact the Yi Dynasty, which has lasted these 400 years, the Crown Prince cannot be allowed to live. Even to make such a suggestion is an outrage and a sin against humanity, and may I never be forgiven.

Lady Sonhui then took to her bed and refused all sustenance.

The King reacted promptly on receiving Lady Sonhui's letter. He announced that he would appear at the Prince's residence within the hour and that the Prince should prepare to meet him. When the Prince received this message, he was uncharacteristically calm. While he dressed in the dragon robe of the Crown Prince, he called Lady Hong to him.

"This is the day I will be killed," he told her.

"No, no your Majesty," she said. "Speak to the King sincerely and he will forgive you. Ask him to help you, to give you more guidance. He cannot refuse."

"He has refused me all his life. What makes today any different? That is not why I called you here. I want to see the Royal Grandson."

Lady Hong trembled at these words but did not show her dismay. "He is with the Royal Tutors," she said. "I will send him to you when he returns."

"Send him to me now!" the Prince shouted. "Don't you understand? It may be the last I see of him!"

Lady Hong then bent her head in grief and left to delay the Royal Grandson as long as she could.

She was helped in this regard by a message which came from the King. He announced that instead of coming to the Prince's residence, the Prince should come to him at Hwinyong-jon Shrine. One would have expected the Prince to forestall, but he did not. He gave in and immediately set off.

I cannot adequately relate the deep anxiety and dread that we in the Palace felt. From the top ministers down to the lowliest of palace workers, none were immune from constant agitation. Now it had reached such a state that King Yongjo and Prince Sado could not both remain alive. And yet, how was it to resolve itself? By law and tradition, a royal body could not be injured even by the King himself.

I accompanied the Prince to the Shrine, walking beside his palaquin, wondering at the fate that caused father and son to act like enemies. What would others who lived after we had died, what would they make of our actions, would they have pity for us or would they blame us for our cowardice?

Even before we came through the gate to Hwinyong-jon Shrine, we could hear the King thundering. He sat on a high seat, a sword in his hand. Meekly, Prince Sado exited the palaquin and knelt before the King.

"You are a disgrace!" the King bellowed. He struck the point of his sword down.

"Father, Father, forgive me," the Prince said. "I have done wrong. I know it. I will change. From this time forward, I will work harder, I will obey you in everything."

The shrine was empty except for the four of us: King Yongjo, Prince Sado, Lord Munno, the King's chief annalist, and myself. Because there were usually many more people about, it felt eerily quiet and peaceful. A flock of magpies suddenly flew up from the wall, all crying out at once. Lord Munno and I looked at each other in terror.

King Yongjo struck his sword down again. With a mighty face, he said, "You are no longer the Crown Prince. You are a commoner. Take off your robe."

Prince Sado turned white, and appealed to the King once more. "Father, please, give me one more chance. I beg you."

But the King's face did not change.

"Don't do this to me!" the Prince cried.

"Will you take off your robe or must I call the Royal Guards?" the King asked.

The Prince stood up awkwardly, nearly falling over so that I wanted to rush over to him. But one look from the King stopped me. The Prince first took off his hat with the jade strings, placing it on the ground, and then disrobed slowly, afterwards folding it neatly and placing it next to his hat. Underneath he was wearing a suit of unbleached cloth, normally worn in mourning. Upon seeing this, fury overtook the King again, and he said, "See? You are hoping to mourn me."

It was just another misunderstanding among a multitude of misunderstandings between Father and Son. We who knew intimately about the Prince's clothing phobias knew that only unbleached cotton kept the Prince from the rashes that tormented him. But there was no way for the King to know this. Ah, what a fate is this!

"You leave me no choice," the King said. "I need to see no further signs of your disobedience." And he called for a rice chest to be brought to the shrine.

The three of us wondered why the King wanted a rice chest at this moment, but of course we could not ask. Prince Sado hung his head and swayed, an utterly defeated boy. The King stood up and paced back and forth, not saying anything further. It was the middle of summer and the heat was extreme. I felt it as a visible presence pushing me down. Thirst plagued me.

In a short time, a rice chest was brought into the courtyard of the shrine. The King told the Prince to climb inside of it.

Surprised, the Prince looked up at his father and said, "No, Father, no. Please, don't do this."

"Get in!" the King thundered, striking his sword once more.

One would have expected the Prince to object further, or run away, or fall prostate on the ground, but he did none of these things. Perhaps he thought it would only be for a short time, that if he showed the King his obedience now, he would be forgiven. But I do not know what truly went through his mind. He simply stepped into the rice chest and sat with his knees up and his head down. The servant who had brought the rice chest then lowered the top. I knew how ever since he was a boy the Prince was afraid of the dark, burning candles all night long. Thus, it must have been terrifying for him to be enclosed in this way. From inside, he continued pleading with the King to be let out, not in an angry, impetuous way, but calmly and beseechingly. It hurt my heart to hear him.

At this moment, the Royal Grandson appeared at the outer gate, crying, "Sire, Sire, please forgive my father! Please spare my father!" He was on his knees, crying very loudly and striking his head on the ground.

"Go away!" the King bellowed. "Leave here immediately!"

The Royal Grandson struggled but he was taken away by members of the Royal Guard.

The King then ordered that everyone leave the shrine, and so we left without the Prince who remained in the confines of the rice chest.

One day passed, then two, then three. From beyond the wall, we could hear the Prince crying out for the King's forgiveness, and then food, and then water. Nothing was brought in.

We were in the middle of a drought, and even in the palace, there was hardly any grass, just pale, sandy dirt outside the stone pathways. How hot it must have been in that prison of a rice chest! How the Prince must have suffered! We went around with heavy, angry hearts, able to blame no one for what was happening. It was all inevitable and preordained from heaven. This King and Prince were born to hate each other. How strange that one was born to the other!

On the afternoon of the eighth day, a storm broke. The sky turned black, roiling with ominous clouds, and a heavy downpour rained on us. Thunder hit with such force that the Palace shook, lightning splitting a tree just inside the courtyard, a large tree that had stood there for centuries. And the Prince, who was afraid of even the character for thunder, how did he endure this terrifying storm? Before this, we knew he was still alive because we could hear him muttering, but after the storm, all sound from the rice chest ceased.

The next morning, the King had the rice chest opened and it was discovered that the Prince was dead.

I tell you this story, Sir, in order that you may know that nothing in life is to be taken for granted, not even the love between a father and son. And that you may know something of our lives here, how we lived, and how we suffered. Do not judge us, nor the King harshly. Because the King had the strength to kill his son, many countless lives may have been spared, as surely discord and chaos would have ensued at the crumbling of the dynasty.

Was our King right or wrong? Hearing this story, good Sir, what might you have done?

---

### AUTHOR'S STATEMENT

Even though the story of Prince Sado is known to most Koreans, I was ignorant of this important historical event because I left Korea before I was old enough to attend school. I moved to America during the time when immigrants tried to fit in by leaving their home countries behind, linguistically, historically, and culturally. My parents encouraged me to speak English rather than Korean out of a misguided notion that it would make my assimilation easier as if nationality was a zero sum game. I could be either Korean or American, but not both. Because of this, I only learned about the story of Prince Sado as an adult when I began exploring my identity. Every country has its own distinct culture and personality. I knew I was Korean but I had no idea what that meant because I was completely unfamiliar with the place itself. How could I call myself Korean if I had no idea what Korea was like, how it had developed, what the people most cared about, or what the nation thought of itself? If you don't know where you come from, how do you know who you are?

I've spent a great deal of my adulthood trying to answer these questions. I studied Korean, traveled to Korea, and read as many books on the history and culture of Korea along with as many translated novels as I could find. I was rewarded in many ways by my research. Learning Korean history filled in many gaps that I had felt were missing. I saw how much of the Korean psyche developed from the fact that geographically, it is a peninsula between China and Japan. Its national identity was forged through multiple invasions from both countries through the centuries, and I finally understood why Korea became the "Hermit Kingdom" as a way to preserve itself.

Along the way, I discovered many interesting stories from Korea, out of which came "The Prince of Mournful Thoughts." On the surface, it's the story of a king forced to kill his son. But, of course, it's about so much more than that—at heart, it's a tragic story of a failed father-son relationship. That makes it timeless and universal, and yet, somehow uniquely Korean in a way I still can't name.

CAROLINE KIM was born in Busan, South Korea, but moved to America at a young age. Her poetry and fiction have appeared or are forthcoming in *Mānoa, The Michigan Quarterly Review, Meridian, Jellyfish Review, Faultline, The Hunger, Five on the Fifth, Pidgeonholes,* and elsewhere. She has an MFA from the University of Michigan in poetry, where she won a Hopwood Award, and was a Michener Fellow at the University of Texas /Michener Center. The fiction manuscript from which this piece is taken is the 2020 winner of the Drue Heinz Prize. She lives with her family in northern California.

# CD Player

**Rachel King**

On the first anniversary of September 11, my dad told me my mom was in hospice. We were eating microwave lasagna while watching the airplanes crash into the towers over and over again. My dad clicked the TV off, then clicked it back on. A commercial for Miller's. "It's serious, Trevor," he said.

I hadn't felt the effects of 9/11 like adults seemed to. I was only eleven when it happened, and I didn't know anyone who'd died in it. Hell, I didn't know anyone east of Idaho. "I'm going to skate," I said.

"Hold on," my dad said. He was switching from graveyard to swing so he could be with her early in the day. He expected me to visit her after school.

"Sure," I said. I rubbed my fingers along the burnt, greasy sides of the lasagna box. On TV, a newscaster was interviewing a kid in New York City.

I skated to Eighty-Second, down to Fremont, then all the way to Rose City Park. I sat on a bench and watched kids finish soccer practice. It smelled like wet leaves and pine needles and car exhaust. I thought about last summer when our old mutt had crawled under my bed and died. I stood up and dropped my board on the sidewalk and didn't stop skating until I was back on Eighty-Second and in front of Joe's, my mom's regular bar. The building's white paint was flaking off. I wondered if Mom's friends there knew where she was.

At home, my dad was getting ready to go work security at Lloyd Center Mall. In the summers, he'd let me skateboard in the parking lot during his shift.

I asked if I could come.

"You have school tomorrow," he said.

"So?"

He readjusted his beanie. "Not tonight, Trevor. Get some sleep."

I watched TV after he left. More 9/11 stuff. I went to my room and fingered a silver CD player and a twenty-dollar gift certificate to Everyday Music, birthday presents from my parents. "I started listening to music at your age," my dad had said. A couple guys who skated were into music but I didn't care about it. Too much sitting still.

I took the MAX, a light rail, to visit her at a hospice care in Northwest Portland. At 3:30, mostly kids rode, but by the time I left Mom lots of people wore suits or uniforms. I hated watching them. On my board I could skate past whoever I didn't want to look at. On the second week of this I brought my gift certificate and took a detour to Everyday Music.

I was rain-soaked by the time I entered the store. The high, whitewashed ceiling felt good after the low, gray sky outside.

"Can I help you, man?" A blue-eyed guy wearing a tight black T-shirt leaned over the counter. His eyes were condescending but kind.

"I'm just looking," I said.

I walked down rows and eyed the CD cases' colorful covers. I hadn't heard of any of them. Maybe my dad had been into music at one time but he wasn't anymore. I didn't know what to pick.

At the counter, the clerk talked to a friend. "Yeah, man, I saw him last December at the Crystal Ballroom," he said. "He was a wreck. He's in rehab now."

"I can't get over *Figure 8,*" his friend said.

"I like *XO* the best," the clerk said.

"Can I help you?" he asked me.

"Do you have that CD?" I asked. *"Figure 8?"*

The two guys exchanged superior glances. I wanted to get the hell out.

"I'll grab it for you," the clerk said. He came back and handed it to me. There was a black-haired guy and a black-and-red skating figure eight on the cover. "You want to listen to it?" he asked.

"I'll just buy it." I held my backpack against the counter with my knee while I searched for the gift certificate.

"Let me know if you like it," the clerk said.

My mom didn't ask why I was late. I don't think she noticed. My dad had brought her a red rose in a tall vase. It was the only decoration in the room. I watched her face while she watched TV. It was pale and her brown hair seemed more scraggly than usual.

At home I put batteries in the CD player. I lay on my bed and listened to the album three times straight. The music calmed me. I didn't understand the lyrics, but one song mentioned skating. I made myself a PB&J, then went to sleep.

I'd never liked school but that fall it was torture. Even before I knew about Mom, I'd decided not to play soccer. When I shuffled by the soccer field after school, my old teammates gave me the finger. My teachers had been "informed of my situation," which meant I had to deal with a lot of sad-eyed looks and talks after class about "doing well in school despite . . ." It was bullshit. I'd never done well in school, and I wasn't doing any worse in seventh grade than I'd done in sixth. I still sat with the skaters at lunch and we told stupid jokes and made fun of each other. I didn't tell any of them about Mom.

The days got shorter and shorter, and I got to hospice later and later because I spent so much time at Everyday Music. Chris, the clerk, let me sample whatever album I wanted, though I bought only used Elliott Smith CDs, and only every couple weeks, when I'd saved up enough allowance. I couldn't stop listening to Elliott Smith. His music was beautiful, and I'd never used that girly word to describe anything. Sometimes I'd ride the MAX all the way to the airport, just listening and listening.

It was weird: while I listened, I was more aware that my mom was sick but it didn't seem as big of a deal or something. It's hard to explain. In the MAX, all the people moved and talked in different directions and none of the movement made sense to me and I didn't care about the people. At home, I hated being alone and TV noise was as bad as people-on-the-MAX noise. Puddles had taken over the city so I didn't want to skate. But Elliott Smith's music made sense to me. The sound was everything I was feeling and had felt, for as long as I could remember having feelings.

Chris liked Elliott Smith's music, too. He'd gone to high school with him, though he didn't know it at the time. He said at one of Elliott Smith's concerts he and Elliott had joked about their old teachers. I was amazed that one day I wouldn't have teachers, that I could get a job as cool as Chris's, one in which I could listen to music all day. I felt stupid for thinking that my dad's security-guard job was cool.

On Sundays, for as long as I could remember, my dad, mom, and I had gone to church, ate at Taco John's on Eighty-Second, then drove around the city looking at houses. Before Mom got sick, my parents had talked about buying a two-bedroom place in East Portland. I liked the idea of living in a real neighborhood with sidewalks. After Mom got sick, Dad and I would drive around Irvington or Ladd's Edition or Eastmoreland. Large houses set back from the street, sidewalks lined with elm trees. My dad was thin and handsome, intense and smart, and when he asked questions real-estate agents responded. But even if we parked our old Taurus a block or so away, they'd sense we didn't have much money. When we walked out the door, I'd feel their pity on my back.

I didn't mind looking at houses we might live in but this was stupid. One day I told Dad that. We were driving down a hill, our car the same pace as the stream of water along the curb.

"I don't want to look at other houses without your mom," he said.

"Why look at any houses?"

"It's fun. Don't you think so?"

I thought about the turrets on the house we'd just been in, about the unfinished basement, large enough for me to skate in. "It makes me wish we had more money," I said.

"You don't have to come along," he said.

After that, I didn't.

One day, after finishing an afterschool detention, I took my first drag on a joint with this skateboarder-turned-prep who hung around after classes like some weirdo. The drag did nothing for me, but when Chris and his friend, Dave, were discussing marijuana, I was glad I'd had experience.

"I'm too old to get high," Chris said. "It was fun in high school. Even in my twenties. Now I'd feel like a creeper."

"Just smoke one with me," Dave said. "You've been so uptight lately."

"Tell me how you feel about it after thirty, Dave," Chris said.

Dave turned to me. I had those large black headphones on; Chris was showing me A Perfect Circle's music. "You want to smoke, Trevor?"

"Don't corrupt the kid," Chris said.

I lifted an ear of the headphones. "I've smoked before."

"See, I'm not corrupting anybody," Dave said. "What'd'ya say?"

"Sure." I set the headphones on the counter.

Chris shook his head. "Not in my store."

"Calm the fuck down, man," Dave said.

At first we stood under the awning, but Chris gave us a dirty look when a customer came in, so we walked down to a green space past Powell's Books, and sat on a wet bench.

Dave was volunteering with a group that was trying to legalize marijuana as a recreational drug. He said people discriminated against pot smokers, but not cigarette or alcohol users. "And it's not even as bad for you."

"People discriminate against alcohol users," I said.

"Yeah?"

I was feeling the effect of the joint. "They didn't give my mom a liver transplant. They said alcohol ruined her liver."

"Yeah?"

I didn't mean to say it. I'd heard Dad talking on the phone to his brother.

"That sucks, man. I'm sorry."

More pity. I'd brought it on myself, and that made it worse. I wiggled my wet butt and kept smoking.

When we were done, I shrugged on my backpack and stood to go.

"Wait, man." He fished in his back pocket and held out his hand. "Save them for a rough day."

He left while I examined three dried mushrooms in a Ziploc bag.

I felt loopy on the ride home—high, I guess—and the *Roman Candle* CD sounded especially good. I'd bought it a few days ago. My Elliott Smith collection was complete.

Right when I got off, I realized I'd forgotten to visit Mom. I stood on the bridge over 205, wondering what to do, feeling rush-hour traffic beneath me. A couple teen boys walked toward me.

"Hey," one said.

I looked away. Only weirdoes talked to each other at MAX stops.

The other snapped open a pocketknife. "Give me your CD player, kid."

I hesitated. He held the knife up higher.

I took out my earbuds and uncoiled the cord from my neck. The guy without the knife snickered when I had trouble untangling it.

I handed it over. "Fuck you," I said. I was still kind of high.

"Watch your mouth, kid," the guy with the knife said. "We're nice robbers. Someone else would stab you." He popped open the case. "Elliott Smith. Cool."

As they stepped off the bridge, their shoulders shook as though they were laughing at something. Probably me.

The rest of the night I lay in bed, staring at the glow-in-the-dark stars my dad had stuck on my ceiling when I was a kid. I tried to stand on my bed and peel them off but I couldn't quite reach. I heard my dad get home and rustle around in the kitchen. He came to my door, a sandwich in hand.

"What's up, Trevor?" he asked.

I didn't respond.

"Buy your mom a fresh rose?" he asked.

"I forgot. I'll do it tomorrow."

"Don't spend the money on music."

The next day I bought a yellow rose at Safeway before I went to Everyday Music. It was kind of wimpy but it was almost winter, I guess. I held it because I didn't want it smashed in my backpack. My hand got cold.

"Who's the girl?" Chris asked.

"My mom," I said.

"Oh." I wondered if Dave had told him about her. "What'd'ya want to listen to?" he asked.

"Some guys jacked my CD player."

"That sucks."

"Can I just listen to one of my Elliott Smith CDs on there?"

I listened to a few tracks off his self-titled. Water dripped from the plastic bag. After Chris had helped a customer, he motioned for me to take off the headphones.

"Here," he grabbed a packaged CD player off the wall. "Pay me back when you can. With your allowance or whatever." He ripped open the package. The CD player was shiny blue.

"Thanks," I said.

I left soon after that. I didn't know what else to say. After I dropped off the rose, I got on the blue line and rode all the way to Gresham. I listened to Elliott Smith's self-titled over and over while passing thousands of houses. Thousands of people could afford a house, but I doubted we'd ever be one of them.

I figured if I never returned to that Everyday Music, I wouldn't have to pay Chris back. There were plenty of record stores on the Eastside. The next weekend I bought a used *Roman Candle* CD at the Everyday Music in Lloyd Center. The clerk there had a white beard and looked like sixty, or older.

The last day before winter break the office called me out of class on the intercom. A couple girls said, "Ooo, Trevor's in trouble." It was embarrassing. I pulled my hood over my head as I walked out.

Dad was on the phone. "Your mom doesn't have much time."

The secretary was staring at me sympathetically so I looked at the clock. It was 1:35.

"I gave you permission to leave early," my dad said.

On the MAX, I listened to *Either/Or.* Something was coming down from the sky but I couldn't tell if it was rain, sleet, or snow. I still couldn't tell when I got outside. I stood under the awning to the hospice entrance and chewed one of the mushrooms Dave had given me. The precipitation looked snow-ish by the time I was done. I chewed another while listening to "Rose Parade." A man in a wheelchair gave me a slit-eyed glare as he rolled himself through the automatic door. I took off up Twenty-Third.

The white lights strung around trees looked blurry. I ogled over a piece of chocolate cake in the window of Papa Haydn's. At Burnside, I crossed the street, then climbed the hill. I was in Washington Park before I knew where I was headed. Mom, Dad, and I used to come up here once a summer when I was a kid. We'd picnic on Kentucky Fried Chicken take-out, then go to the rose garden or zoo.

As I passed swings on which Dad had pushed me super high, the CD skipped, then died. Stupid batteries. Snow was falling harder. I couldn't hear anything—no cars or barks or voices. At the rose garden, I walked alongside the bushes while chewing on the last mushroom. Only a few roses were in bloom. The rose festival queens' names were carved into the brick path. My mom had said she'd wanted to be a rose-festival princess in high school. I wondered if that would have changed her life. If good things like that change your life or if you're always going to be who you're going to be no matter what happens.

Larger snowflakes fell more quickly. I pissed on the names of the princesses. This was the best moment I'd have for a long time. Mom was dying, or already dead, and everything was fucked up. I zipped my jeans, then saw more roses. Red, pink, and yellow, on every bush all over the garden, the smallest as large as my fist.

---

## AUTHOR'S STATEMENT

I babysat, nannied, coached, taught, or mentored kids almost continuously from the time I was eleven until I was twenty-five. Trevor, the main character in "CD Player," is a composite of different boys I worked with. I had a soft spot for his kind: a loner from a possibly unstable background who had trouble knowing how he felt. I myself came from a stable family, but could be a loner and—like more boys than girls, perhaps—had difficulty articulating my emotions. When I found a poem, character, or song that embodied my feelings, I would, like Trevor, read, view, or listen to it over and over.

I wrote "CD Player" during the decade I lived away from my home state of Oregon. Sometimes in winter, when I missed nineties Portland, I would watch the Elliot Smith music video "Lucky Three," and the puddles, bridges, roses, and warehouses—as well as the music—would comfort me. For the first time, Elliott Smith's music and Portland became intertwined, and I thought of when I had discovered his music, and the process of discovering music as a child or adolescent, often while going through a difficult time and/or puberty.

In addition to paying homage to Elliott Smith and portraying a boy discovering music, "CD Player" explores how art can sustain and enlighten, while at the same time removing a person from family members or others who care for him. I think it was necessary for Trevor to latch onto music at this time in his life, but I hope that in the future he'll also return to his relationship with his dad, the clerks at Everyday Music, and his skater friends, just as I hope those loner boys I worked with have learned, as I have, how to live in intimacy. But their present-day stories, including Trevor's, I can only imagine.

**RACHEL KING**'s short fiction has appeared most recently in *One Story, Green Mountains Review, Lunch Ticket,* and *Pigeon Pages,* and has been nominated for a Pushcart Prize and Best of the Net. Her poetry chapbook, *Between Work and Light,* is available from Dancing Girl Press. In her fiction, the characters are always paramount, but her stories and novels also explore exile, past trauma, workers' rights, and land-use issues. She lives in her hometown of Portland, Oregon. Find out more at booksrachelking.com.

# To My Unborn Son

**Pat Matsueda**

*an apology*

Years ago yes I could have had you
You could have been born and stretched
my world around you

A life doesn't happen that way, though
Desire grows on a thought, a feeling
and extends itself, trying to grasp
what it wants

But if thoughts and feelings remain captive,
bound by debasement, poverty,
loss, coercion,
then desire doesn't form properly

It doesn't snare the light and dark,
properly braid the soft and strong,
tough and yielding
How little I understood,
myself ill formed

I had to protect you
in the non-space of being
the space of non-being

where your potential was unrealized,
unhurt by time

My perfect boy, I protected you from life

## AUTHOR'S STATEMENT

The word apology has two meanings: acknowledging and expressing regret for an action; and, as the alternate form of apologia, defending one's actions. I called "To My Unborn Son" an apology because I wanted to draw on both meanings, believing they are two parts of a whole intention.

Deciding not to have a child after conceiving it is a conscious act that, to some people, requires acknowledgement and expression of regret. In the case of my poem, the soul to whom the apology is addressed is the unborn child and the apology comes decades after the act.

Someone once said that there are two kinds of truth: a simple one, whose opposite is false; and a complex one, whose opposite is also true. In "To My Unborn Son," I tried to create a complex truth: that deciding not to have a child—sparing him the trauma and injury that will likely be his life—is an act of love and compassion.

PAT MATSUEDA founded the Ms. Aligned project, which seeks to help the genders understand each other through the writing of women. She is the managing editor of *Mānoa: A Pacific Journal of International Writing* and the author of *Stray*, a collection of poetry, and *Bedeviled*, a novella. With Lillian Howan and Angela Nishimoto, she produced the 2019 issue of the University of Hawai'i ezine *Vice-Versa*.

# Crocodile Teeth

**Donna Lee Miele**

We were the ones who found the abandoned boathouse upriver of the delta. Most people had better places to go. Even Edward and I wouldn't have started hanging out there if not for the way things were—him with his sister running things at his grandma's place, me with my dad out to get me all the time. We were always looking for a place of our own, and no one else wanted the boathouse. It had fallen out of use since the mining operations upriver had moved away, and the canoes were no longer needed to guide the barges through the shallows. And it was beyond broken since the storm, which had carried away most of the canoes. But one end of it was packed with sacks that someone had left behind. The sacks turned out to be stuffed with teeth. Edward said they were crocodile teeth, and that the poachers shot last year in the raids must have lived here. I wasn't convinced. The teeth were so small.

"Baby crocodiles," Edward shrugged. "Easier to catch."

We took the teeth to an older guy who made bracelets for the tourists. He made a ton of rosaries, naturally, out of the local seed pods, but had recently become known for merchandise featuring sharks' teeth. He was impressed with our teeth. He said they were a good size for bracelets and anklets. Any bigger or sharper and the tourists tried to return them because the teeth bit into their ankle bones and the soft skin on the insides of their wrists. Sometimes they called the cops on him when he refused to refund their money. One time, he'd even had to disappear for a few days. I heard it was because a foreigner had lost a foot or a hand after getting an infection from one of his shark's teeth, which he'd gleaned from a half-eaten carcass he'd found on the beach.

"Piss-bleeders," he called the complaining tourists, as we negotiated our sale of the first handful of crocodile teeth. "They want to wear *teeth* because it's so hard belly and then they crumple like a pinched tit when the teeth act like teeth!"

"We found hundreds," I said. He wanted to come and see.

"Better that we bring them to you," said Edward. "They're embedded in the foundation of a poachers' house. It's tight in there and might be dangerous if you don't know your way around."

I watched the guy's face go reptile—still and blank. Even I could see, in my mind's eye, the newspaper photos of the poachers' bodies after the raid. They were probably more torn up than even that beached shark's carcass.

"There are a lot of teeth," Edward said, "but it takes hours to even get a little handful like this."

"Okay," grumbled the guy. We left him sitting on the wall overlooking First Beach, along with all the other vendors and smugglers gathering for the tourists. Straggles of groggy, newly arrived beachgoers were already having umbrellas set up for them in front of the hotels.

As we jogged away, Edward said, "Couldn't let him go stealing all our teeth."

"How'd you know he would?" I said.

"You know how it is," he said. "Finders keepers. If he knows where the boathouse is, he goes back there without us, he gets to keep what he finds." He told me about the box of candy his sister had gotten from a tourist who followed her home—or maybe it was a local guy, one of the hustlers who sell sneakers and sunglasses, stuff stolen off the beaches. Anyway, it was real Belgian chocolate, each piece shaped like something different, roses and whelk shells and foreign tree-nuts. When Edward had asked for some, his sister had teased payment from him for every piece, making him do this or that chore before she gave it. He finally found out where she kept the box, and just ate the candy all in one sitting. "She was so mad," Edward said. "But she couldn't do anything about it because it was gone."

I was scared of Edward's sister. After Edward's parents got lost looking for work upriver, she took over their grandma's house like she'd just been waiting for the chance. She bullied Edward, she bullied their grandma, and she even bullied the guys that started hanging around, who offered everything from repairs to the wornout old house to actual money for the chance to date her. They thought she'd be easy because she and Edward were orphans. She didn't even pretend to be nice to them. She had a look so cold she could make the bag shrivel between your legs.

If you were one of those guys, and you tried to come up on her grandma's veranda, she would stand on the edge, look down on you, and say something like, "Take yourself to the beach and remember me to your family," meaning Last Beach, though even she wouldn't say that right out. Last Beach is full of whores of every kind; and every one of them, of course, is someone's family.

Edward's sister scared everyone, not just me. It must have shown on my face because he said, "She didn't even really care about the chocolates. She hates sweets. She just yelled at me and whupped my butt once, and that was it. It was kind of funny actually."

Edward and I had it good for a while. The bracelet guy gave us ten percent of what he made on the teeth merchandise, which wasn't bad. The crocodile teeth bracelets, for instance, sold for double the price of rosary bracelets, even though the crosses and angels he bought cost him more than our teeth.

"Everybody's got rosaries," the guy said. "Genuine crocodile teeth, that's rare. That's powerful."

"I don't think they're crocodile teeth," I said, but Edward told me to shut up, and the guy didn't listen to me anyway.

It didn't take long for the guy to get greedy. He and a couple of other hustlers, all three of them bigger than Edward and me, followed us to the boathouse one day. I got slammed through one of the rotting walls and stayed down even though I wasn't knocked out. Maybe that's what money in your pocket does, makes you tender and unwilling to fight; or maybe when you're a slacker and a loser like me, you take as few hits as possible because you know that in days to come you're going to get hit again, and worse. But Edward fought them even though he was half their size and outnumbered three to one. One last hit to the gut finally forced all the breath out of him. He buckled and curled up at their feet. The guys took the teeth. That was that.

I crept back in to find Edward in the sandy litter on the floor. He held his stomach and struggled to breathe, making a croaky, rasping noise like the things that live under rocks and hide in the nighttime delta trees. He took so long to breathe right again that I panicked and, loser that I am, started to cry.

"Why fight them, Ed?" I moaned. "We got plenty of money off that guy. At least he's not making us give it back."

"*We*. Found the teeth. Stupid. It's finders keepers!" He couldn't make talking and breathing work together. "And. The hell d'you. Mean. Plenty of money?"

I didn't know what I meant. I'd never had money to spend before and had no idea what to spend it on. It had been accruing in my pockets ever since the first sale to the guy. I did know that if my parents ever found it, they'd take it. They'd have probably taken the teeth too, just like our business partner had. I'd been saying all along that the teeth weren't real, but that didn't matter. The fantasy was the idea of being able to keep anything valuable a secret in the river delta.

Edward had a bruise on his cheek and a long, thin cut along one thigh where a tooth had sliced him as he'd struggled to keep hold of the last sack. I was stiff along my whole right side, where I'd hit the wall. I couldn't put weight on that hip. We had to hold each other up, each with one good leg.

When I got Edward home, his sister got one look at him and slitted her eyes at me. I stammered out the whole story. She took Edward into the house without even offering me a drink of water, but okay. I didn't deserve it. I limped home and slept badly. I kept dreaming of creatures with lots of teeth—sharks, crocodiles, even things I'd never seen, like vampires and wolves. I was always one of the beasts, but my teeth kept crumbling.

---

## AUTHOR'S STATEMENT

I have an anklet made of hematite beads with a single crocodile tooth. I got it from a hustler in Palawan, Philippines, where tensions run high between crocodile conservation efforts and human comfort. On this resort island on the South China Sea, white-glove service and fulfillment of a tourist's every last desire have probably been the rule for as long as there have been tourists and desires. There are a lot of such areas in the world—where the resort beaches wear the white gloves, and the beaches in between resorts strip down to nothing but hustle.

That sounds harsh, doesn't it? But children grow up in such places, so there's play in the hustle, and in case you're thinking that hustlers are whores, most of them are not. Most kids grow up playing along with the hustles of their elders, and one day find themselves self-reliant.

My own grandmother learned her hustle in the Philippines early in the twentieth century, after "graduating" from a Presbyterian orphanage, where she was placed not long after the Spanish-American War. She found her way out of economic want by selling foodstuffs—and probably trinkets, just like the guy who sold me my hematite beads with the single crocodile tooth. My father was a hustler, too, growing up during the Great Depression in New York City, and his labors varied from shining shoes to working for pushcart vendors to hauling ice.

Depressed economies twist families; and men, as the traditional heads of household, are often the unfortunate faces of families distorted by economic challenges. My grandmother went into the orphanage after her mother's second marriage—whether because her stepfather would not take her in or for some other familial war-related trauma, no one knows. My father was the first person in his family on either side to graduate high school, but his father would not pay for him to go to college, out of pride in a peasant's existence: if the strength of his back, a roof over his head, and a hot dinner at the end of the day were not enough for a man, he was, in my grandfather's judgment, something less than a man.

But boys. From my own boys, who've grown up never wanting for a thing, to my father as a seven-year-old shining shoes for nickels—they don't have to become twisted. Too often, somewhere along the line, someone calls a boy Loser, whether it's his own father or someone else, and after a while, the nickname sticks. It doesn't have to. It's likely that Edward's friend in "Crocodile Teeth" earns the nickname Loser from his father, but I can allow myself to imagine an alternate home in which the father, to make light of a failed effort, gently calls his son Toothless, and welcomes him back. You can survive and thrive without teeth. I don't think you can survive the conviction that, in a world of winners, you are destined to always choose the loser's hustle.

And just to be clear, the Filipina grandmother I'm talking about was my mother's mother. My father's people came from Italy's war-stripped countryside, about a hundred years ago. So far, I've failed to talk about about why I write what I write, but any consideration of why I do anything always comes to this: trying to hear the ongoing conversation among my people clearly, from a place deep inside me. They are voices from opposite cheeks of the globe, generations removed from each other, but they're talking about the same world. It's right here.

DONNA LEE MIELE plays with characters, settings, and conflicts that evoke her mixed heritage and her parents' experiences of war. While she also writes historical fiction, she finds greater freedom to explore (and greater fun) in stories with less concrete settings, which was her intention with "Crocodile Teeth." She hopes that readers will enjoy playing in this fictional intersection of contemporary Southeast Asia and the Depression-era United States. Her stories have appeared or are forthcoming in *|tap| litmag, Atticus Review,* and *Red Fez,* and she is a founding member of River River Writers' Circle.

# Sex Education: A Tragicomedy, Part II

**Angela Nishimoto**

## BROTHER (1962)

Mommy had Mark. After they came home from the hospital, Mommy leaned over the crib. She was happy. She said to me, "I want you to see. He's a boy." She beamed.

I knew there were boys—there were some in our neighborhood. But Mommy said, "Watch." She unpinned Mark's cloth diaper and showed him to me.

On tiptoe to look into the crib, I said, "What's that thing?"

Mommy said, happy, "'At's how he makes shi-shi. Boys and girls make shi-shi differently."

*'At's why Mommy likes him more'n me,* I thought.

## DING-A-LING (1966)

Wendy and me went to the Hashimotos' house next door. Our brother, Mark, was there, playing with Hiram Hashimoto in Hiram's room. They'd been in the small, round, plastic pool, their swim trunks still damp.

I was inspired. "Let's play Ding-A-Ling!" I said.

"What?" Wendy said.

The boys looked intrigued. I explained, "You pull down your pants. Like this." I wiggled my behind. "And yell, 'Ding-a-ling-a-ling!'"

I demonstrated, pulling down my pink shorts.

"Okay!" Hiram said.

"Let's do it!" Mark said.

"Okay," I said. "One, two, tree!" We pulled our pants down and wiggled our butts. "Ding-a-ling-a-ling!" we shouted. We looked at each other, laughed. Then we pulled our pants up.

Then we did it again.

Then we did it again.

A knock on Hiram's door. Mrs. Hashimoto said, "What're you doing?"

Hiram said, "Nothing."

She knocked again. "Unlock the door."

Hiram did so, and opened it, looking at his feet.

Mr. Hashimoto was behind Mrs. Hashimoto. They looked down at us.

Mr. Hashimoto said to me, "You and your sister go home. Boys should play with boys. And girls should play with girls."

## MAY DAY (1967)

We were in fourth grade, covering Hawaiian Culture in Social Studies. Our class went on a field trip to the Kamaka ʻUkulele Factory in town. We found out how much one Kamaka ʻukulele cost. Fifty dollars. "Wow!" I said. "Expensive!" The man giving us the tour gave me a sour look.

For the May Day festival at school, we practiced playing "Pearly Shells" on our ʻukuleles. We played and sang.

I hung around with Johnny Henssen. He was tall and had a really big stomach. Johnny had a blond crewcut. He and his parents came from the Mainland. The other kids whispered that he stank. I wondered if he took a bath only once a week—like Huckleberry Finn. I didn't know that much about *haoles,* though I had cousins who were *hapa-haole.* I finally decided that *haoles* take their baths on Saturday nights only.

Johnny took me to his house after school once. I met his mother, Mrs. Henssen. She was tall, fleshy, and smiling. She gave us butter cookies and milk. I gobbled the cookies because I was unused to snacks after school. I was hungry for more, but I knew that I would be a pig if I asked.

We played Scrabble. I won one game and lost another.

I thought it over. I was Japanese-American, and I would marry a boy of my own kind. Johnny was *haole,* and some of us local kids hated *haoles.*

On May Day, the boys wore Hawaiian print shorts and went bare-chested. Girls wore *muʻumuʻus.* All of us were bedecked in plumeria leis, their fragrance sweet.

Johnny, taller and bigger than all the other kids in the class, and me, one of the smallest, strummed our *ʻukuleles.* Johnny smiled, plucking at his instrument.

I looked at his fatty titties and suddenly felt revulsion. I said, "You stink!"

He stared at me, burst into tears, then swung—and *bong!*—knocked me in the head with his *ʻukulele.*

Marina, nearby, said, "I'm telling Mrs. Oshiro!" Our teacher.

I said, "No, no. That's okay." I put my hand where it hurt, on my temple. My head throbbed and I felt faint. "No need." I felt sick.

"I'm telling." She left.

Johnny went to the principal's office.

I felt so bad about turning on Johnny, who'd been nice to me, and kind—unlike other people. What was in me, that I'd do that to Johnny, who'd been so friendly? *He's a* haole*—and he stinks.*

I did the May Day performance in a daze and didn't respond to other kids' expressed concern. I figured that I'd deserved it.

For several days I had a knot on the left side of my head. I never told my mother, or anyone else in my family, ashamed of my cruelty.

## NAMES (1968)

Boys called at each other when there was conflict in elementary school. No racial or racist slurs—as far as I knew—except for *haole* and black people. All the other kids there were some kind of local: mixed ethnicities, *hapa,* or "pure."

At times, a boy gave chase and the guy fleeing stopped running and flashed a V with his index and middle fingers: *Peace, brah.* The pursuer often gave it up.

Boys name-called when they wanted to insult. Frequent appellations: *punk, homo, faggot, girl, sissy, panty, muff,* etc.

It felt personal to me.

## DANCING (1968)

Mrs. Yamada taught our sixth-grade class in all subjects: reading, writing, arithmetic, history, social studies, science. She had us dance for physical exercise. Many of the boys seemed uncomfortable, but gamely, grimly, put their best feet forward.

We met in a darkened, downstairs classroom and waltzed or square-danced to music played on a phonograph. I was usually paired with Daniel because I was the smallest girl and he was the smallest boy. Sometimes his hands were sweaty. Sometimes we changed partners.

*A heel and a toe, a heel and a toe, and slide, slide, slide,* the hokey, folky-sounding man sang. We girls and boys would move to the left in the double girls-facing-boys circle and come opposite a new partner. Most of the boys had been in our classes up the grades, from first to sixth, so I knew them. Some partners were more graceful and better dancers than others, of course. A few of the boys seemed to hate dancing, but all the girls enjoyed it.

I had a flaw: I had a tendency to try to lead when dancing even though I was a girl. That was a no-no. Nevertheless, despite admonitions from Mrs. Yamada, there I was, trying to lead Daniel in a waltz. One-*two-three,* one-*two-three,* one-*two-three,* Mrs. Yamada called out to the music.

Daniel attempted to lead me; I tried to lead him. We struggled. I pushed him on the shoulder; he pushed me back. I kicked him in the shin. Hunching, he grabbed my right hand in both of his and bit me hard.

"Ow!" I yelled, snatching my hand back.

Mrs. Yamada broke us up, and Daniel sat out the rest of the period at the principal's office.

Next day, Mrs. Yamada joked about who should lead in dancing and said that "Angela kicked Daniel—and he bit her right back!" She laughed, along with the others in the class—except for me and Daniel.

Later in the term, Mrs. Yamada was excited that we were going to dance to what she called rock music. We didn't have to touch sweaty hands, or get out of the way when our partner misstepped. Mrs. Yamada announced that she would throw a party at her house, and we had class periods when we'd develop and practice our rock dancing. Mostly we'd dance to "Take a Letter, Maria" by R. B. Greaves or songs by the Jackson Five, Michael Jackson fronting the family group, singing lead vocals. The songs had an energetic, young beat, the music more pop than rock.

About this time, I listened to Top 40s music on the radio, Station Six-Nine, KKUA. We'd be going to intermediate school the following year, "A big change," Mrs. Yamada said. "There'll be dances at King Intermediate," she told us importantly.

We had a month to learn to rock dance. I told my mother about it because she was going to have to drop me off at Mrs. Yamada's house. Mrs. Yamada said we had to be creative in our dancing. "Unlike square-dancing, you don't want to look or move exactly like someone else. Strive for uniqueness."

I think most of us didn't get it. But we tried our mightiest to dance. Mrs. Yamada encouraged us to watch *American Bandstand* on TV for inspiration. She seemed so excited.

Mom sewed for me a sleeveless black top and beige-and-black-patterned bell-bottoms for the shindig. She bought me black square-toed flats with brass buckles. Mrs. Yamada distributed invitation cards for the event. I'd figured out a way of dancing that wasn't the same as anyone else's style. It featured taking big steps forward and backward.

The Saturday afternoon arrived. Mom dropped me off. We ate cold-cut-and-cheese sandwiches and drank sodas. Then Mrs. Yamada put music on the phonograph and said, "Come on, boys!"

The boys asked the girls to dance.

We danced, self-conscious in our fancy clothes, trying to look cool and mod. I loved my new clothes. It was a great time to be young.

---

**AUTHOR'S STATEMENT**

"Sex Education: A Tragicomedy, Part II" is an excerpt from a longer work begun a few years ago. The piece grew and grew, breaking my personal memory walls with its power to remind me about what happened so long ago. The whole work is comprised of short, discrete scenes that seem to end up as a story of my sexual education. Sex was all around, of course, as it always is, but at the time I was growing up in the 1960s and 1970s, nice people didn't talk about it, at least not out loud. Whispers and hints about sex and its power dogged my psyche. What was unsaid seemed more important that what people articulated, even in undertones.

The longest of the pieces in *Ms. Aligned 3* is about betrayal. Betrayal of a friend and betrayal of the self. I really liked the boy because he was nice and kind to me. I ended up siding with the group—most of our class—in my renunciation of that big, blond, haole boy. And have regretted it ever since.

I Googled his name and found someone living in Hawai'i, married to a Japanese woman. I don't know if this man is the grown-up boy I remember so vividly and with such regret. Wherever he is, I hope he has a happy life.

Bless you. I'm sorry.

It can take a lifetime to figure things out.

**ANGELA NISHIMOTO** holds an M.S. degree in botany from the University of Hawai'i at Mānoa. She grew up on the windward side of O'ahu, teaches on the leeward side, and lives in Honolulu. She writes fiction, nonfiction, and poetry and has published extensively, but not exclusively, in Hawai'i. Her work can be found in *Hawai'i Review, Hawai'i Pacific Review, Kaimana, Bamboo Ridge, Ms. Aligned, Writing Raw,* and elsewhere.

# Family, Family

**Jeannine Ouellette**

The thing about Leo Whittaker is that although he was not liked, he was not unlikable, as some children certainly are. Grown ups, especially teachers, won't always acknowledge this, and I don't particularly care to acknowledge it myself, truth be told. But it's a fact—some children are simply foul. Not Leo, though. Not at all. Leo was just a bird-boned slip of a boy with blue veins pressing through his clear skin like a curvilinear map of rivers. He was a placid child who committed none of the usual offenses that tend to mark first graders. He neither picked his nose nor pushed and shoved the girls, nor licked the bottom of his shoes, nor tugged at his penis absentmindedly throughout the school day. And even for a first-grade boy, Leo wasn't the slightest bit dirty or smelly—although, to be fair, none of our students at Rolling Meadow Waldorf School were dirty or smelly. They were too well heeled for that. Some of our families did reject chemical deodorants—so inevitably those children would ripen by sixth or seventh grade. But I digress.

If anything, I found Leo more charming and likable than most seven-year-olds, what with that sweet, clear diction of his, those dark raisin eyes, that uniform of green corduroy pants (green "for grass" and corduroy "for the extra nice feeling of it") and bright argyle sweaters. I admired his tidy lunches of almond butter on sourdough, dehydrated pineapple wrapped in waxed paper, and glass jars of sauerkraut. (Homemade: his mother also fermented her own sourdough starter, yogurt, and kombucha.) Speaking of fermentation, Leo shared his mother's knowledge of the art and science of it, on which he sometimes expounded. "In Latin, ferment means to leaven," he told me early on that September. "That word is old-fashioned," he explained. "It means to wake up. Or turn something into something else."

Leo was an advanced reader in first grade, which set him apart, because we didn't formally teach reading at Rolling Meadow until second grade or even third. We felt it was better overall not to pressure children too soon with abstract academics. But Leo already had the key to the kingdom, and was often absorbed in one of those *Eyewitness Books* about Egypt or wild animals or what have you. And then there was his fascination with our dolls, those sweet flannel things stuffed with clean wool, their round heads sewn perfectly smooth and faceless—all the better for imagining—and framed by silky, close-cropped hair. "Dolls are for Little House," the other boys often chided Leo. And it was so: in our school, dolls did belong primarily to the Little House—that's what we called the low, asymmetrical nursery-school building on the east side of our grounds. The Big House, a two-story brick building across the field, held classes one through eight, or—as we all said simply—"the grades." The Big and Little Houses were separated by a hundred yards at most, but Humboldt's cosmos may just as well have lain between us as far as the children were concerned. After all, the Little House was for making porridge and playing house and napping on cots in the afternoon, a soft babyish place filled with soft babyish toys, while the Big House was for real school, a place of wooden desks and chalkboards and days filled with numbers and letters and lesson books. The only real remnants of the Little House in our first-grade classroom were those three special dolls, hand sewn and ferried over in Moses baskets by the Little House teachers on the first day of school—as a blessing. As I have said, Leo found them enchanting.

But neither his love of the dolls nor any of his other habits made Leo unlikeable—not even his kraut, despite the smell. (Foster Cross loved sardines; Maisie Bishop ate Vegemite with crackers; and Jeong Malloy, whose American parents had adopted her from Korea and were intent on raising her in what they considered a culturally sensitive manner, brought kimchi at least twice a week.) No, the kraut was not the problem. The problem was that Leo—I don't know how else to put this—was simply different. And children are not typically keen on difference, especially when they don't have a word or a label for it, which was the case with Leo. You see, at Rolling Meadow, we frowned on labels. We believed children should unfurl like ferns—organically, according to their own timetables, no hothousing. All would work out as long as the child wasn't forced to bloom on a schedule.

And we were right about this in many ways. But not all.

In defense of Leo's classmates, I should point out that Leo shared virtually none of their interests or passions. To their beloved handclapping games—Miss Mary Mack and Say, Say Oh Playmate—he would shudder and pull away. "I don't *like* the feeling of skin," he would insist. "Especially on other people's *hands*." Rope-skipping contests? Leo could stand neither the texture of the hemp rope nor the sound of it slapping the asphalt. Hopscotch and jacks were also out—the *sweating*, the *touching*. But Leo did take a shine to one of the first-grade games—the one game, in fact, that eventually became the whole class's favorite, Family, Family. This oddly repetitive name belied a byzantine and shape-shifting world of make-believe invented and governed by the children themselves.

At first, I thought Family, Family was just a more complicated version of house, in that it involved mothers, fathers, and dolls as babies. But it soon became clear it was more than that. The children played during recesses and lunch and breaks and every other spare moment. They even, when they could get away with it, played the game during our lessons. Indeed, they played Family, Family everywhere—the classroom, the grassy field, the woods—but of course, our special dolls were not allowed outside. "Who cares?" Lila Baxter said. "We'll be our own babies!" And so they were. And at the outset, roles and family units reshuffled moment by moment. *"I'm* the mom now," a big sister might shout to her uncle, "and *you* can be my baby!" Leo preferred being a dad, with a parenting style tailored to his own aversions and phobias. *"No, no, no!* Don't touch her *skin!"* he'd scold. Or, "For heaven's sake, put your sweater on before you catch your *end*." Some first-grade babies very much enjoyed Leo's fretting and vied for him as their father, to his surprise and delight.

Soon, however, families concretized. Most were headed by a mom and a dad, but one had two moms and Leo was a single father. Regardless of their makeup, once families were set, they were set. The only way then left into the game for the few children with no other role was to be a baby, which is what became of children like Travis and Cara. I believe this was also when Foster Cross called for an end to Leo's turn as a dad. "You're hogging," Foster said. "But I guess you can be a baby…if you want."

Baby Leo especially liked Lila as his mother, but he was quickly traded away to Jeong and Maisie. Then came the day Darren demanded that babies no longer walk or talk. "That's *more real!"* he said. Negotiating the rules of Family, Family took up more time than the actual playing of it, primarily because no one was remotely in charge of the thing. Lila had invented it, but her authority had collapsed almost instantly. Therefore, she had no real say about the rule that ultimately banned babies from choosing their own parents, leaving them at the mercy of being chosen or not, and thus paving the way for orphanhood.

Which is exactly what happened to Leo.

In those first glossy weeks of September, the three Little House teachers tried to warn me. They would cross—when their own morning lessons were over—that dry Sargasso Sea of flattened grass to the Big House and float curiously past my classroom like fairytale mothers. We all thought of them that way, with their long skirts and aprons swishing just above the polished tile floors. They would peer into my classroom—or, if my door was closed, gaze through its small square window. On many occasions, I felt a hot prickling of nerves down my neck and across my clavicle bones, only to look up and see the uneven floret of their narrow faces at the glass, which by then would be fogged with their breath as they strained to see how their little ducklings were faring under my fledgling wings. You see, not only were the first graders new to the Big House, but so was I. It was my very first year of teaching: these children and I were just beginning what was to be an eight-year voyage. At Rolling Meadow, as at all Waldorf Schools, teachers in the Big House pledged to teach the same group of students not for just one year or two years, but from the first day of first grade all the way through to the eighth-grade graduation. Imagine: one teacher with the same children for almost a decade. We practically raised them! It's no wonder the Little House teachers were nervous for me. It's no wonder I was nervous for myself.

Of course, I already lived and breathed Rolling Meadow by then, with my own sweet son Henry having begun in the Little House five years earlier, when he was barely three years old. Just a baby! Though of course like most mothers, I was foolish enough at the time to think three was a big boy. Now, at eight and a half years old, Henry was in second grade, the classroom next door to mine, with Mr. Whittaker, Leo's dad, as his teacher. This is how it was at Rolling Meadow, all of us teaching each other's children like one big family. In our brochures, we even touted how our teachers were like a second parent or a favorite aunt or uncle. Of course, anyone who has actual parents or aunts or uncles knows this can go many ways. For my part, I was relieved that Henry was in Thomas Whittaker's class. Thomas Whittaker had been at Rolling Meadow longer than any of us. He had already taught one group of children all the way through eighth grade, then he'd done the same with a second group, and now, with Henry's class, he was on his third time through the eight-year cycle.

"We're too lucky," I always told Whittaker. And it was true. Parents in Whittaker's class tried and failed to disguise our smug expressions of having drawn the long end of the stick, of being astonished by our own dumb luck in a place where everything was supposed to be fair and equal. Mrs. Pinter, on the other hand—our fourth-grade teacher—was clearly not cut out for the job. *Shoddy,* we would whisper about her students' paintings hanging in the hall. *They're not even trying for her.* Likewise, the parents in Mrs. Pinter's class made little effort to hide their hangdog disappointment over their assigned teacher. Frankly, they displayed dread, like people watching from the porch while a green sky sucks itself down into a funnel. "What if Henry had ended up, by the fault of astrology alone, in Mrs. Pinter's class?" I would sometimes joke with Whittaker. We all gossiped this way about each other. But there was nothing in it. At Rolling Meadow, we teachers taught in freedom and governed ourselves—we were even called a Circle of Teachers, deciding all things in a collective and nonhierarchical manner. No principal to quash our creativity! In this environment, to openly criticize a colleague was not only awkward, but a bit like asking for it yourself, if you know what I mean. Besides, Mrs. Pinter's daughter, Polly, was in my first-grade class. Which is exactly my point: all of us at Rolling Meadow were woven together like a tapestry. And Thomas Whittaker was a golden thread among us.

But of course, what I was trying to tell you about was the Little House teachers, and how they warned me.

"Oh, Leo Whittaker," the Little House teachers chirped to me that autumn when we passed one another on the play yard or in the faculty room. "He's a bit of a gray duck, isn't he, Ms. Mallery? Keep an eye on him, won't you?" And I tried. I did. But all through September, I couldn't catch my breath long enough to truly *see* anything. I hadn't yet gotten my "classroom legs." That's a sailing metaphor, but what comes to mind when I think of that time is not exactly the sea, but something less poetic—that pure bastard child of the American gambling and entertainment complex known as the "money blowing machine." Imagine being shut into one of those contraptions with the clear glass walls and powerful fans. Dollar bills swirl while you flail and contort yourself to catch one, two, maybe even five if you're agile and lucky, before the wind dies. But then imagine that the wind never dies, and instead of dollars, it is children slipping through your fingers.

When the month of September finally snapped its mouth shut, it was on the day of our annual Feast of St. Michael festival, or Michaelmas. I watched my first graders gallop around the field clutching tinfoil swords in their fists, yellow gauze capes flapping behind them, the girls with blue asters braided into their hair. Parents milled about in pairs and clusters, stirring stone soup and ripping apart steaming round bread loaves and slicing Granny Smith apples for dipping into raw honey. Eventually all of the children sat down on the grass, dipping and chewing and waiting for the dragon—a giant silk puppet carried by the eighth graders—to slink out from the woods. For St. Michael—usually played by Mr. Mark, our beloved woodwork teacher—to stride out from somewhere on the other side of the chicken coop and the gnome house. Until recently, St. Michael's job was to slay the dragon to a grisly death, but changes to the script now required him to extend his sword stoically and tame the beast nonviolently instead. The children, being children, were nonetheless bloodthirsty, and stiffened in anticipation of the kill—cheeks bright with the heat of the afternoon, fingers sticky with honey—as all around us, swerving drunkenly through the air and in the dry grass, came the bees, golden and heavy with the change of seasons, wings glinting in the thin light, stingers ready, mouths searching.

With the unfurling of October, we fell into a rhythm. Our little boat righted itself, and it might have sailed smoothly, had it not turned out that my seasickness was not all from teaching: I was several weeks pregnant. This turn of events was abysmally timed, what with me being right at the outset of the eight-year pledge. Of course, there was no rule about getting pregnant—life happens—but still, you can see how the timing was not ideal. Yet the first-grade parents were gracious enough, truly they were. And I imagined the children themselves might be rather excited at the news, what with their obsession with Family, Family.

I decided to make my announcement to the class first thing on a Tuesday morning as my students were filing into their rows of desks—Sun Row at the front of the room, Planet Row at the back, Moon and Star in between. "Circle, circle, round and true, you see me and I see you," I sang out as I drifted to our large braided rug next to the cubbies and sat myself down cross-legged, tugging my blue wool skirt around my knees. The children formed a lopsided circle around me, wriggling forward in anticipation of what fun might lie ahead now that they had been called unexpectedly away from their desks. When they were all wide-eyed and quiet, I whispered, smiling broadly all the while, that I was going to have a baby in the spring. I looked from face to face. "Ms. Mallery?" Travis said finally. "Is it snack time yet?" Cara, who had been picking away at her elbow, held something up. "Foster!" she shouted. "I got the scab!" Only Leo widened his eyes and tilted his head until his ear nearly grazed his shoulder. "A baby?" he whispered back to me. Leo Whittaker, it soon became clear, was *smitten* with the idea of my unborn child.

Had the advent of my pregnancy—or at least, my knowledge of it—not coincided more or less with the birth of Family, Family, I may have been more aware of the slow unraveling of that game, who was being let in or left out of it. As it was, I was mostly focused on keeping my breakfast down while staying ahead, or at least not too far behind, with my lesson planning. You might be shocked at the great effort and time it takes to memorize all of the fairy tales and songs and number games and so forth that make up a first-grade day. Besides that, I can't deny how charmed I was by Leo's heartfelt fascination with all things related to my baby. "Ms. Mallery," he said one day during lunch, not long after he was apparently orphaned in Family, Family. He was standing at the corner of my desk, eating his dried pineapple. "Do you think your baby *can* see us from inside you? Around your belly button, where the skin is thinner?"

"We can't know for sure," I said. You see, Waldorf teachers don't believe in quashing the magical ideas of children too soon.

"I hope your baby can see me," Leo said, "because then it might know me better when it's born."

Another time that October, Leo drifted over during knitting hour—an hour that was especially trying for him. Not only could he not keep left straight from right, he also confused the back leg of the stitch with the front leg and the over the fence with the under. Mrs. Olson, our handwork assistant, was constantly helping him to cast off, untangle, and begin again, and Leo was losing motivation to care about the scarf he was failing to produce as he watched his classmates' rows of red and yellow and blue grow stripe by proud stripe. So he drifted. "Ms. Mallery," Leo said to me that day. "My dad says babies are boring when they're brand new. *Extremely* boring. Is this true?"

I laughed. Thomas Whittaker, twice divorced, had two grown sons from those earlier marriages—but his third and current wife, Nan, had desperately wanted a child since she hadn't yet had one. Hence, Leo. "Well," I said to Leo, who was gazing up at me so expectantly with those dark raisin eyes, "I think newborn babies are quite magical, because of how pleasant they feel in your arms, and how delicious they smell, especially their fuzzy heads. And because of how they look at you in a peculiar way, as if they have been searching the wide world for you forever with their deep-ocean eyes. But it's true that they can't walk or talk or play with toys—or, really, do much of anything other than sleep and eat and dirty their diapers. So, some people might call them boring, yes."

"I guess I can't know how boring they are until yours is born," Leo said. "But when your baby grows big enough to *for sure* not be boring, I'm going to teach it all about the whole wide world. Also, I'm going to give it a present." With this, he patted his argyled tummy. That's when I saw how he had stuffed the waistband of his sweater into his corduroy pants—how the sweater bulged out. "I'm growing a baby," Leo said, catching my gaze. "A baby for your baby. See?" He pulled the neck of his sweater out and reached down to extract a mass of brown and purple yarn. It vaguely resembled—if you *really* used your imagination—a small doll.

Over the next few days, Leo divulged more and more to me about his yarn baby. "She's a girl," he told me. "Because I hope you have a girl. But even if you have a boy, I will be his friend." Leo's baby was made of the longest unbroken strands of discarded wool yarn he had collected from his many false starts on his scarf, those discards he'd stuffed into the bottom of his calico knitting bag. In that sense, Leo had fashioned this baby from his own failures. "I think I might wait to name her until your baby is born," he said. "But I have six ideas so far for names in my notebook. For now, I call her Yarnie." At all times, Yarnie stayed under Leo's argyle sweater—except overnight, when she slept inside his knitting bag in his cubby to "keep us all safe." Leo told me as much one afternoon while he watched me drawing a mountain on the chalkboard, its two purple peaks forming a perfect capital M. "But that's a secret, Ms. Mallery. Don't tell *anyone*. Because Yarnie is special. She's like the starter in sourdough—or the mother in kombucha. She has extra life in her."

Here, he paused and leaned far forward, resting his elbows on my desk. "And just because she's made out of yarn doesn't mean she's not real," he said. "You told us real is whatever we believe in."

I didn't think of myself as betraying Leo when, during recess that afternoon, I said to Thomas Whittaker—we were leaning against the woodshed drinking coffee and watching the children play Simon Says—"I take it you and Nan aren't trying for a second?"

He pretended to choke. "Why would you ask such a thing? Just because you have a tadpole, you're free to ask such things?" He gave my arm a little pinch. Suddenly, he looked his age, or older. Softer. No one would say Whittaker was attractive, really. At least, I wouldn't: those saggy corduroy pants (apple, tree), the thinning comb-over. The Adidas with ragg wool socks. The one missing molar and the hole it left behind next to his lower left canine (to be fair, visible only when he laughed). Whittaker himself had attended a Waldorf school in California—the only one of our faculty who had. Maybe that's why the women of Rolling Meadow were so enchanted with him. And that was another thing about our school: the way we could flirt a little without being taken the wrong way. Whittaker was like my older brother. There was no danger in it.

"I'm not trying to be nosy," I said. "It was just something Leo mentioned. About babies being boring."

"Oh, I was just squelching his latest obsession."

"Babies?"

"Mating. Those *Eyewitness* books have got him asking questions—extremely literal questions."

"I guess that explains his interest in my baby."

"I didn't realize he had an interest."

"Well," I said. "He's making a—he says it's a present for my baby, for when it's born. But it seems more like some kind of poppet."

"A poppet?"

"You know, those folk-magic dolls—Middle Ages stuff—for protection and whatnot. He keeps it in his sweater during school. You haven't seen it?"

"No," he sighed. "I most certainly have not."

Days passed before the other children noticed Leo's baby bump because, for the most part, they took little notice of him in general. But it was inevitable that they would finally catch wind. Children always do.

"Leo has a *baby* in his sweater," Foster Cross told the class one Thursday after painting. "He doesn't know boys can't have babies!"

"Leo doesn't even know he's a boy!" yelled Darren, rocking from foot to foot.

"I don't believe he *has* a baby in there," Foster said. "He's just *pretending* to have a baby 'cause he thinks then he can be a dad in Family, Family again. But he can't! Leo, you *can't!* So show us, Leo, if you really have a baby. Show us!"

"Yeah, Leo, show us!" Darren said.

*"Show us! Show us!"* the children chanted, their clear soprano voices dipping half an octave from the villainy of their demand.

"No," Leo said, backing away. "I can't. She's not born yet."

"Children," I said, clapping my hands. "That is enough. Anyone in our class who *wants* a baby *can* have a baby, including Leo. And Foster, if you so dearly want a yarn baby, you can make one of your own." He didn't, of course. Because Leo already had. Instead, Foster's interest in what was under Leo's argyle sweater grew more intense.

Leo took to wearing a belt with his corduroys—a wide, khaki web belt that cinched his pants so tightly around his waist that the corduroy formed pleats. He spent more time by himself in the book nook and the sandpit. "Ms. Mallery?" he said one recess, just as I was getting ready to ring my cowbell to line the children up. Leo was digging a tunnel aimed for South America because, as he explained, this would avoid the Earth's molten core. "Ms. Mallery?" he said that day. "Growing a baby is a little like fermenting, isn't it?"

"Not exactly," I said. Leo's face crumpled. "But I'm no expert, Leo, on babies or fermenting."

He stood up then and wrapped his arms around his plump sweater belly and suggested that Yarnie, while not a traditional name in America, could be a real name, if we said it was, because people were making up new names all the time. "Ms. Mallery, do you like the name Yarnie?" he wanted to know. "Do you think it's pretty?"

One afternoon at the end of October, I came back to our room after Miss Marla's Spanish lesson—she was teaching the children a darling verse for our Hallowmas festival the next day—only to find Leo at his desk in the middle of the second row, rocking back and forth in his chair. The other children had formed a circle around the outside of the desks. "Throw it to me!" they shrieked. And "My turn!" and "Now me!" Cara was jumping up and down and grabbing at the air and then clutching her fists to her chest, and Foster was snatching back at the air, screaming, "No! I caught it!" All of them were jumping and throwing and grabbing frantically at nothing at all.

"What in heaven's name is going on?" I said. But none of them even pretended to stop themselves. My voice had lost whatever slim magic it ever had.

"Throw it this way!" Maddy yelled.

"No!" Darren yelled back. "You dropped it already! Do you want Leo to get it back?"

"You're all lying!" Leo cried, slapping his palms on his desk. "You don't have her! None of you do! She's *not born yet!*"

"First grade!" I yelled, my voice higher and shriller than I ever liked for it to be. "To your seats, now!" I began rubbing the palms of my hands together, and Lila Baxter, bless her heart, began immediately to do the same. Her eyes looked heavy, about to spill, and so I rubbed my palms faster and harder, and soon half of Sun Row had joined me—Milo and Jeong and Cara were already in their seats and the others were filing in too—and the sound of their hands was lovely. I began to snap my fingers, left and right, and the children in Moon Row, behind Sun Row, followed suit: Travis and Katie and Polly, but not poor Leo, whose head was on his desk. By now the children knew exactly what was happening, and they were all scrambling to their desks. Foster was climbing over Ian and Maisie in Star Row to get to his seat faster, and just as he plunked himself down, I looked straight at him and began to clap my hands, while the children in Sun Row continued rubbing their palms together, making that nice soft whirring, and those in Moon Row continued snapping, and only in Star Row did the children clap with me, softly at first, but then with more and more force, until finally I looked to the very back, Planet Row. I began stamping my feet then, and those children followed suit, stamping harder and harder, until the symphony of wind and rain and thunder we were conjuring became so transfixing, so hypnotic, that the temperature in our classroom dropped by several degrees and the scent of wet pine rose from the skin of our palms, and we were in awe of ourselves, and we never, ever wanted it to stop.

When I entered the classroom the next day—Hallowmas morning—Leo was on his knees facing his cubby, shoulders quaking. A small group of children swarmed around him.

"Leo, what's wrong?" I said, kneeling down.

"She's gone." He swiped at his eyes with the backs of his hands. "Yarnie is gone." Leo's calico knitting bag lay on the floor in front of him, inside out.

By now some of the girls had also begun to cry. Maisie and Jeong were searching under pillows in the book nook, and Lila was trying to rub Leo's back even as he scooted away from her. "We'll find your baby, Leo," Lila was saying. "I promise we will." I suggested we check every child's knitting bag one by one, just to make sure the baby hadn't gotten into one by "mistake." Bag after bag turned up babyless.

Finally, I had no choice but to usher the children to their desks for our morning verse. They tromped single file, heads hanging, into their celestial rows. Then they dutifully crossed their arms over their chests. All but Leo. He stayed on the floor by his cubby, crying quietly. "Children," I said. "I am so very disappointed. I cannot tell you how disappointed. I can only hope that Leo's yarn baby will find her way back into his knitting bag by the end of this day. If that happens, everything will be wonderful in our classroom. Everything will be forgiven without question. If, on the other hand, Leo's yarn baby does not come back today, you will stop playing Family, Family forever. Do you understand?"

A wave of nods passed through the field of their faces, catching briefly on the empty spot where Leo should have been. We stood for morning warm-ups, and when we were finished, I got out our basket of colored beeswax. Surprisingly, Leo loved the beeswax as much as the other children did—for its smooth warmth in the hand, its sweet smell, and the way it could be shaped into tiny animals, trees, and even people. Still, he would not budge from where he knelt by his cubby. So the rest of the children pulled sullenly at their wax until I passed the basket to collect it again.

Only when we lined up to go outdoors for pumpkin carving did Leo finally raise his eyes to mine. "Will the second grade be outside, too?" he wanted to know. The promise of seeing his dad always buoyed him.

"Yes," I said. "All the grades will be carving pumpkins for the festival."

With that, our whole class, including Leo, lined up two by two.

The play yard was a blur of commotion: the middle schoolers armed with Sharpie markers and safety carvers helping the younger children draw their desired jack-o'-lantern faces and then attempting to produce something resembling that vision. I waved at my Henry, but he was too deep in concentration to wave back.

"Don't you love Hallowmas?" I said to Whittaker.

"I do," he said. "I especially love seeing these cool eighth-graders elbow deep in pumpkin guts." He aimed that at Paul Libby, the decidedly uncool but kind eighth-grade boy helping Leo. Paul was scraping out piles of orange gunk. No pumpkin guts for Leo's delicate hands.

"He had a rough morning," I said.

"You mean that yarn doll? I'm kind of relieved. That was getting too weird."

"It was kind of weird," I said. "But it was sweet, too, the way he carried it in his sweater like that. I have a hunch who took it."

"Forget about it," Whittaker said. "I know I sound cold hearted, but you have to take the long view. That ball of yarn was not making his life easier."

"Oh, but Thomas, that little yarn doll meant something to him. It was so ... Leo."

"Would you feel the same if it were Henry, digging in the sand alone at recess with yarn stuffed down his shirt?"

"Okay," I said. "I do see your point. But still, I think it was sweet, and I believe Leo *will* find his way with his classmates, eventually. With or without his Yarnie. I know he will—all of them will."

As we spoke, eighth graders began dragging the tarps to the dumpsters to shake off the slime. The three Little House teachers helped carry the finished pumpkins to the back entrance, exclaiming over them. "Aren't you a handsome fellow?" and "Oh my, what a scary face you have!" They even gave the pumpkins little kisses to "bring them to life" before lining them up cheek to cheek beside the door.

I wandered away from Whittaker to admire the finished jack-o'-lanterns for myself—the traditional gap-toothed smiles were my favorite—before drifting deeper into the play yard toward a gathering of first graders that looked, I realized with a stab of anger, a lot like Family, Family. Especially since Travis and Cara were crawling on the ground, and I knew them to be babies. I was about to ring my cowbell to break up the game when I spotted the purple yarn vining through the grass like a stem of pokeweed. I knelt down and pulled at the strand. It drew easily from one side, so that soon I had gathered it several feet to its end. I followed the rest of it in the direction it led—away from Family, Family, away from the center of our grassy field, toward the north end of the grounds. I followed it and followed it, pulling and winding the strand into a ball that grew larger and rounder as I went, until finally I came to the shallow kidney-bean pool outside the henhouse, with its floating lilies and water lettuce, its three iridescent koi fish and, in the narrow end of the bean, where the branches of the small willow swept across the surface of the water, the last sodden ends of Leo's yarn baby, tied in a clumsy bow to the end of a long tendril.

I cannot remember now if the first graders were still playing Family, Family when I cut back across the center of the grassy field. To be honest, I don't recall any children on the field. I remember walking alone. But that can't be right, because recess was not over. I had not rung my bell. I would not, in fact, ring my bell. The other teachers would eventually ring their bells, and my students would come running with the children from all the other grades. They would scramble into two straight lines right next to Mr. Whittaker's students, and Mr. Whittaker would cover for me, as we sometimes did for one another. He would start counting the heads—second graders first, then my class. But almost as soon as he began counting, he would already know, and Lila would already have told him, "It's Leo, Mr. Whittaker! It's Leo who's gone!"

By then, I would already be in the Little House—now empty for the day and eerily quiet—breathing through the sharp cramp coming over me and inhaling the scents left over from the little ones' morning: the warm comfort of oatmeal, cinnamon, and chamomile; the earthy cloves from the "kitchen corner" with its wooden play stove and round table and perennially favorite tool, the mortar and pestle; the strange and sulfurous smell of the Prussian-blue watercolor paint that never quite dissipated between painting days. I made my way down the cool, dark hallway, past the children's little wooden cubbies—their hand-painted nametags so delicate and sweet, this one with a nest of tiny robins, that one with a wide-eyed baby fox—and into the main nursery room. That's where, when all the little ones went home at noon, the dollies then slept together until the next morning, swaddled in plain cotton blankets and tucked neatly into their pine cradles. Except now the faceless babies were strewn askew across the wool rug and their cradles were empty, save for the one pushed up against the gauzy pink curtains of the north window. There, curled tightly on his side, breathing softly, argyle sweater untucked, wet stockinged feet hanging over the pine footboard, was Leo, his face smooth and pale, staring blankly at me.

---

## AUTHOR'S STATEMENT

> *This is Earth. It will never be heaven. There will always be cruelty, always be violence, always be destruction.* Rebecca Solnit

When I was in second grade, I lived in Douglas, Wyoming, with my mother, stepfather, and two sisters. At the time, we attended a Lutheran church, because my mother had been excommunicated from Catholicism as a result of divorcing my father. This was the early 1970s. We eventually stopped attending church altogether, but for that year in Douglas, we were Lutheran, and over Christmas, my Sunday School class held a gift drive for orphans abroad. I don't remember where abroad, just abroad. I do remember deliberating long and hard about what I should bring to that gift drive.

On the one hand, I wanted to give something wonderful, something an orphan would really love. In other words, something I really loved. On the other hand, my family was chronically broke and we didn't have much ourselves, so it was hard to let go of something I genuinely cared about— like, say, the little box of costume jewelry I had dearly wished for, bravely asked for, and, to my utter surprise, received as my absolute best Christmas gift that year. I had no idea the jewelry was essentially worthless. To me, it was glorious. So, to give the shiny drugstore ring and bracelet, or to keep them? This was the question, and I struggled long and hard before accepting that I had no choice. After all, this was church. God was watching.

When I arrived at Sunday School on the morning of the gift drive, carefully wrapped and taped jewelry box in hand, curling ribbon spilling from its corners, I watched in horror as another little girl from my class skipped up to the orphan tree with an unwrapped box of Colgate. Indeed, several boxes of toothpaste sat under the tree, alongside packages of diapers! I was appalled. What poor orphan would want toothpaste or diapers for Christmas? But when I expressed my righteous indignation to my mother, she said those were the items orphans needed most. The lights on our tree flickered. I pictured my precious, useless jewelry jostling on the back of a truck, headed for parts unknown.

That gift drive was one of my first conscious encounters with the intricate relationships among wishes, ideals, intentions, and reality in this complicated world. Since that initial disillusionment, I have maintained my ideals while falling short of them repeatedly. Still, my aspirational fire, especially for personal development and social transformation, burns on, as does my curiosity about the chasms between idealism's bright air—so thin, so high—and the hard ground we walk on, with its thick grime and mottled scars. Most of all, I am fascinated by what can grow and fester in those chasms, especially power imbalance and abuse.

This particular fascination catalyzed my novel-in-progress, from which my story, "Family, Family," is excerpted. Ultimately, "Family, Family" places children in a make-believe world of their own creation, a world wherein they test the limits of their own principles and power. Leo, the little boy at the center of "Family, Family," defies the familiar tropes of masculinity and, therefore, male entitlement. He is bird-boned and slight, eschews ruckus and roughhousing, is averse to touch and texture, reads voraciously, and prefers the company of his pregnant teacher to that of his peers. Perhaps most dangerously of all, Leo flagrantly disregards gender norms by carrying an unborn "yarn baby" of his own under his signature argyle sweater.

Not coincidentally, "Family, Family" also takes place in a Waldorf school, where ideals are high indeed, and based almost wholly on the vision of the schools' founder, Rudolf Steiner, who genuinely wished to transform society for the better by establishing a new social order that would recognize and nurture the spiritual nature and development of human beings. Many of Steiner's ideas are beautiful. Some are problematic. Either way, real-world implementation is challenging. During my ten years as a Waldorf elementary- and middle-school teacher, I witnessed the mayhems, small and large, that erupted when human error and imperfection, including my own, clashed with the expectations of a hyper-idealistic closed community. My own children are Waldorf educated, and I maintain much respect for the artistic principles and transformative striving of the education, but I am also curious about how our ideals can inadvertently propel us headlong into trouble. In fact, that's exactly the kind of trouble that interests me most.

Ultimately, then, "Family, Family" and much of my work tries to tease apart stubborn knots in the threads of idealism—and not just the knots found "out there," but also "in here," where my own heart twists and strains.

**Jeannine Ouellette**'s memoir, *The Part That Burns,* is forthcoming from Split/Lip Press in 2021. Her essays and short stories have appeared widely in journals, including *North American Review, Calyx, The Writer's Chronicle, Penn Review,* and others, as well as several anthologies. Her work has earned two Puschart Prize nominations, fellowships from Millay Colony and Brush Creek Foundation for the Arts, and recognition in many contests, including the Iowa Review Awards, Calyx's Margarita Donnelly Prize, Bellingham Review's Annie Dillard Award, Cutthroat's Barry Lopez Creative Nonfiction Award, Narrative Story Contest, december magazine's Curt Johnson Prose Awards, Proximity's Essay Contest, and The Masters Review Fiction Contest, where "Family, Family" first appeared as the second-place winner. Jeannine teaches writing through the Minnesota Prison Writing Workshop, mentors through the Association of Writers and Writing Programs, and is the founder of Elephant Rock, a creative writing program based in Minneapolis, where she lives near the banks of the Mississippi. She earned her MFA in fiction from Vermont College of Fine Arts and is working on her first novel.

# Want in the Third Grade

**Connie Pan**

You were my ex's friend, taller, quiet
to his loud. You lived three playgrounds away.
We met at borders, where our parents allowed

us until sunset. The way you looked
into me glittered my everything, but
you couldn't because *loyalty.* I can taste

that eight-year-old regret, remember
the mourning. What a tiny kill. Never had
I thought you would like me. My first

lesson in romance, at least something
I could control: never accept a first
offer. I clench my teeth over how many

decades it takes me to learn. *Be picky,*
I tell every child I know. Because it's likely,
the silhouette you adore on the outskirts

of conversations—barely smiling, never
a *Hi*—loves you and writes your initials
inside the bands of their underthings, too.

**AUTHOR'S STATEMENT**

In February 2016, I drafted a series of poems, including "Want in the Third Grade," in a fury. My reading records from early that year say Maggie Nelson's *Bluets* and Roxane Gay's *Bad Feminist* swam and somersaulted in my brain. Revisiting that time in my journal, I admired the moon; I dreamt of glass shattering, cigar smoking; I made salads while listening to writing podcasts; I watered aloe vera and orchids while lizards skittered, snails ambled, and a pigeon family in the eaves across the lawn talked; I scheduled a hair appointment for March, my first balayage. I miss the town house with the big windows that I drafted these poems in. I miss the built-in desk that overlooked the parking lot, where I wrote, where—later—I watched people carry away the things we couldn't sell or bring with us across the Pacific.

For three years, I let those drafts simmer. After spending two years in California, working 9-to-5s, cohosting a wedding with my love, stealing writing time, driving cross-country with plants waving in the truck bed, I—in Mississippi—opened the proverbial drawer to revisit the little things that emerged from what I can most aptly describe as a painful emptying. I understood little about this poem—and its sisters—other than I knew I had to write it after seeing it there.

With *Ms. Aligned 3*'s theme of childhood lending candlelight, I recognize that at this poem's heart lingers a smarting regret alchemized into love: the impulse to share a hard lesson in the hopes of lightening the weight for another. It wants to be a tender nod across the room or a kind, welcome hand on a slumped shoulder. I may not be a mother, but I have been mothered, have mothered, and I keep returning to something Chani Nicholas wrote: "What you heal in yourself you heal for your entire family line."

**CONNIE PAN,** originally from Maui, earned an MFA in fiction from West Virginia University and a BA in creative writing from Grand Valley State University. Her writing has appeared in *The Fiddlehead, Carve, PRISM international, Rosebud Magazine, Bamboo Ridge,* and elsewhere. An excerpt from her novel-in-progress was nominated for a Pushcart Prize. A freelance writer and editor, she lives in Mississippi.

# Staying Open

## An Interview with Ann Pancake

In the good Granma smells Mish stands, the nighttime powder, the church perfume. He tumbles with his fingers the man in his pocket. His daddy peels the foil from the tiny package he has taken from Gran's dressing table drawer. Daddy, his hand tremoring, fishes in the package's dropper of water, snares the lens on a finger and daubs it at his eye. Mish watches. Not out of curiosity for the contacts, those he has seen his whole life, whenever Daddy can get them, Mish looking on from the low single bed at Daddy's house, bedtime, get-up time, Daddy picking plastic in and out of his eyes, Mish is used to that. He watches for the funniness of Daddy at the dressing table, where Granma puts on her makeup, combs her hair. For the strangeness in Gran's mirror of Daddy's raggedy-brimmed Stihl cap, his penny-colored beard. With the effort to keep his eye open, Daddy's top lip is raised, and in the mirror, Mish can see the two big front teeth browning from the middle out, like a banana left too long. Then the lens pops in, and as though having the thing in his eye grants him the gift of seeing behind, Daddy turns.

from "Me and My Daddy Listen to Bob Marley"

### INTERVIEWER'S NOTE

In 2016, Ann Pancake was selected as the first recipient of the Barry Lopez Visiting Writer in Ethics and Community Fellowship, administered by the Mānoa Foundation, an educational nonprofit organization in Hawai'i that is copublishing this volume of *Ms. Aligned.* As part of the fellowship, she gave a community address on the social responsibilities of artists and writers, speaking gracefully and forcefully. (Interested readers can find the speech online at manoaethicalimagination.wordpress.com.) The following year, she taught creative writing at the University of Hawai'i at Mānoa and read "Me and My Daddy Listen to Bob Marley" at a department event. I was deeply impressed by the powerful way she captured the thinking and behavior of a young boy beset by family difficulties. In this edition of *Ms. Aligned,* I'm happy that we can share her philosophy of writing and her generous spirit.—P.M.

**PAT MATSUEDA** This new volume in the Ms. Aligned series consists of writing by women about the childhoods of males. Your story "Me and My Daddy Listen to Bob Marley" is an inspiring, captivating tale about a boy who has a speech impediment that prevents him from correctly pronouncing words, including his name. But he possesses the magical qualities of childhood: he knows how to play and imagine, and he has a strong desire to grow and learn. Though he lives amid dreary circumstances, including the drug life of his father, he has a fierce light inside him. Can you tell us what inspired you to tell this boy's story—and to open the world he lives in to our eyes?

**ANN PANCAKE** I was inspired to write this story because the boy and his father are closely based on my nephew and my brother. To be honest, I think writing the story was an attempt to work through my own trauma of helplessly watching my nephew undergo his trauma.

Initially, I tried to write the story from the first-person point of view of an adult who was more or less me. After many failed drafts of that version, I was rereading Faulkner's *Light in August,* one of the scenes where Joe Christmas is a little boy. The voice and the emotion of that scene moved me to try the story of my nephew from his point of view as a four-year-old.

Beyond the specific and intimate story of my nephew, I wanted also to open to readers the world of so many children in Appalachia who are innocent victims of the opioid epidemic. I now teach at West Virginia University, where I have students who were those children and who are now, nevertheless, making amazing lives for themselves. I notice that some of these former victims have amplified powers of empathy, intuition, and insight because of their experiences.

I wrote the story around 2007 when my nephew was six and I was looking back on his life when he was four. My nephew is now 18. He's become one of the former victims I describe above: his life is still not at all easy, but he has amplified powers of empathy, intuition, and insight.

**PM** Dan Chaon has said, "In her unflinching and lovingly accurate attention to the lives of the working poor, people who have fallen entirely beneath the radar of our literary notice, [Ann Pancake] occasionally calls to mind the haunting photographs of Walker Evans...but I don't think there's anyone else like Ann in American letters." In honor of such literary work, you became the first recipient of the Barry Lopez Visiting Writer in Ethics and Community Fellowship. Given what you know about communities like those in "Me and My Daddy," how do you fortify yourself to write with accuracy and love?

**AP** I rely on a strong spiritual practice to sustain me. I don't really want to talk about that! But the truth is, that's my primary source of fortification.

Also, I grew up in a middle-class family, but I grew up in communities where most people were working-class or poor. Now I live again in a working-class WV community. So, I have lifelong experience of knowing these people, going to school with them, and having them as friends and neighbors. I know deeply and I know firsthand the ways these communities are full of love, care, decency, integrity, and forms of wisdom that aren't necessarily valued by middle-class urban people. I also have a lot of knowledge of the history of Appalachia and of West Virginia in particular—specifically, I have a lot of knowledge about the exploitation of Appalachia—so I have a broad perspective on the reasons for despair, addiction, and bigotry in the region. I guess all of that fortifies me, but the bottom line is, I love the land here and I love the people here, despite all the hurt. Maybe I love it all even more because of the hurt.

**PM** What kinds of advice do you give to young writers—male and female—when they are trying to render a male character's interior self? His feelings about himself, his world; his expectations and hopes.

**AP** First, I would recommend that the young writer read like crazy, all kinds of literature, to get an idea of the many different ways authors have rendered the interiors of human beings, especially human beings different from the authors themselves.

Next, I would recommend that the young writers step outside themselves—put the self off to the side—and climb into the body, the mind, and the heart of the male character. Once you locate yourself inside the boy or man, try to move through the world from deep inside that character, seeing as he would, feeling as he would, listening as he would, thinking as he would. You might, to practice, just give yourself a scenario to play with—say, place the character on a short journey and see from the character's perspective as you write that journey. Or put the character in a party and write the party from the character's first-person point of view. This can teach you even if you don't end up using it in a piece.

Give yourself time. Give yourself room to experiment and play and mess up. Don't rush it. Write many drafts. Don't think too hard during those early drafts.

If you run up against an obstacle—let's say you run into a situation where you have no idea how the character might act or react or WHY the character might act in a particular way—you can always talk with boys and men who might have greater insight to offer you. For example, when I wrote my novel about mountaintop removal, I had a boy character who was in love with four-wheelers and with big mining machinery. I had no idea how a person could love big mining machinery. So I did a few interviews with men I knew who love big machines—and they made it make sense to me.

Take risks. Stay open to what your characters are showing you. Listen. Don't impose your self.

ANN PANCAKE grew up in Romney and Summersville, West Virginia. Her first collection of short stories, *Given Ground,* won the Bakeless award. Her other books include the novel *Strange as This Weather Has Been* and *Me and My Daddy Listen to Bob Marley: Novellas and Stories.* She has received a Whiting Award, NEA fellowship, Pushcart Prize, and creative writing fellowships from the states of Washington, West Virginia, and Pennsylvania.

# Teddy

**Grace Loh Prasad**

They all said it was a terrible idea. "Are you sure?" asked Eldest Sister, who is my best friend. She's the one everyone listens to and looks up to—including me—but this time I stood my ground. For once I didn't care if she or anyone else disapproved.

My whole life I've been a model of responsibility and good sense, and you know what? It's not a recipe for joy. I follow the rules. I never eat more than half a bowl of rice because I'm diabetic, although lately I allow myself a small bowl of red bean soup, or a tiny piece of cheesecake, no bigger than two fingers. I deserve to live a little, don't I?

Against everyone's advice, I adopted a puppy. I did it as soon as I got home from the hospital—that way nobody could say no. My sisters were so happy and relieved when I was discharged, and they didn't want to upset me in case I got sick again.

I've always wanted a dog, ever since I was young. I love their happy energy and natural curiosity. All my life I've been constantly on the move, always traveling for work, so having a dog was out of the question. But now that I'm retired and home all the time…Why not?

The puppy is about three weeks old according to the pet store. He's a small dog with a wedge-shaped head, short, curly black-and-white fur, and a very cute face. In Taiwan, the name for this kind of dog is 迷你雪納瑞—a transliteration of the English name "mini Schnauzer." The breed is sometimes called 小雪 for short, a nickname that means "little snow." Many people also call this breed 老夫子狗, which means "old master dog" or "old scholar dog" because of its conspicuous white beard and eyebrows which give it a thoughtful and serious expression. So of course this is the perfect dog for me, a lifelong scholar.

I named him Teddy after my son Ted, who died four months ago.

Ted was only forty-six years old when he joined our Lord in heaven. He left behind a wife and three school-aged children, and because they live abroad, it's much harder for me and the other relatives to help them. He left no savings, no life insurance, nothing to sustain his family. He never thought about the future, only the present, and look where that got him.

Of course, it wasn't his fault. Cancer is nobody's fault. I wish I could have done more for him, other than loan him money. Sometimes it was for school tuition; sometimes for rent. Over the last few months, it was for his medical treatment. I never said no. It was both too much and not enough. No matter what I did, I could not save him.

I was at Ted's side when he took his final breath. He was delirious, writhing in pain, going in and out of consciousness. I asked him if he believed in God, and he said yes. An existential weight was lifted from my shoulders, but in its place was the heaviness of responsibility, of figuring out how to support his family after he was gone.

But I don't want to talk about that, I want to talk about Teddy…Eldest Sister is fretting about where I am going to keep a puppy in my small apartment and who is going to take him out for walks. I'm sure Mina can do it; she can walk him and take him out to do his business when she goes to the market to buy food. Teddy is so cute, so bouncy and full of joy, that I'm sure everyone will want to pet him wherever Mina takes him. So what if it takes her a little longer to do all the errands. I don't mind.

My dear wife Lucy doesn't really like the puppy, but she doesn't object to it either. We've been married for almost forty years. Ten years ago, Lucy was diagnosed with Alzheimer's, and she barely talks anymore. For a few years, the disease made her anxious and paranoid, and she kept trying to run away, so we moved her to a nursing home for her own safety. I used to visit her for three days every weekend, and spend the rest of the time at home. But after a couple of years, those symptoms went away, and she went from being panicked and disruptive to being completely passive and docile. So I brought Lucy back home with me. Now she mostly sleeps or watches TV.

She didn't come with me to Ted's funeral. She can't travel anymore, and what would have been the point? Even if I explained to her that our son had died, she would neither understand nor remember it, and it would only compound my grief to have to tell her over and over to no avail. I guess it's better in a way that she doesn't realize Ted is gone. Although she is no longer capable of having a conversation, she communicates through her eyes. From the way she looks at me, I know she recognizes me and feels safe.

Why does an old man like me want a puppy now? I'm seventy-five years old, about to turn seventy-six. I can't even run after him. My Parkinson's has gotten worse, and I can only walk very slowly, with help. I just got out of the hospital. They never figured out what the issue was other than the panic attacks that started after Ted died. They taught me how to breathe into a paper bag when

I start feeling anxious and breathless. The doctors say I'm fine, that there's nothing really wrong with me, but my heart feels weaker. I think my body is slowly breaking down.

The truth is I'm really in no shape to take care of anyone. I look after Lucy, but mostly we depend on other people to take care of us. Mina lives with us and takes care of the washing, cooking, cleaning, shopping, and making sure we take our medications. Eldest Sister and her daughters visit and check on us almost every day. Lucy and I would not be able to live at home without their help.

By adopting Teddy, I've simply added another dependent to the household, another being who requires care and attention and cleaning up after. Was it a selfish decision? Perhaps. But I feel I don't have much time left. I don't want to have any regrets.

I'm surprised by how much I love Teddy already—his tiny tongue licking my face, his stubby little tail wagging back and forth, his inquisitive little face. It doesn't matter to me if he's clever or well behaved. He does tend to bark a lot, so we'll need to work on that. He's not very obedient, but I don't mind.

Ultimately, the dog has only one purpose: to be loved.

All I ask in return, Teddy, is that you don't die first.

---

### AUTHOR'S STATEMENT

My older brother Ted was hospitalized in September 2010 after chemotherapy and an experimental surgery failed to defeat his aggressive liver cancer. I made an emergency trip to Bangkok to see him one last time and pleaded with my dad, who lived in Taiwan, to join me. My dad almost didn't come because he was ailing from Parkinson's and had a lot of mobility issues, plus my mom was deep in the throes of Alzheimer's and needed twenty-four-hour care at home. In the end, I convinced him to come. My dad arrived in Bangkok first, chaperoned by my cousin, and I arrived a day later—but it was already too late. Ted passed away while I was en route, and the purpose of my trip changed from saying goodbye to attending a funeral.

A few months later, I found out from my aunt on Facebook that my dad had adopted a small puppy and named him Teddy, after my brother. I was horrified—it felt strange and wrong to name a pet after my brother, not to mention highly impractical for my dad to get a puppy in his advanced age and poor health. But it was too late to talk him out of it. He had just returned home from his own hospitalization and was in no shape to care for anyone else, and on top of that he was worn down from years of caring for my mom, in the late stages of dementia.

I was upset with my dad for doing something so impulsive, but what was the point of criticizing him in the depths of his grief? "Teddy" was my attempt to see from his point of view, to imagine the heartbreak of losing his son and the added pain of not being able to turn to his wife for comfort or solace, and his only daughter and all of his grandchildren lived in other countries. I imagine Teddy was his last desperate attempt to feel some joy.

**GRACE LOH PRASAD** was born in Taiwan and raised in New Jersey and Hong Kong before settling in the San Francisco Bay Area. She received her MFA in creative writing from Mills College and is an alumna of the VONA workshop for writers of color along with residencies at Hedgebrook and the Ragdale Foundation. Her essays have appeared or are forthcoming in *Longreads, Catapult, Jellyfish Review, Ninth Letter, Blood Orange Review, Memoir Mixtapes, The Manifest-Station, The Rumpus,* and *Cha: An Asian Literary Journal,* and she is a contributor to the anthology *Six Words Fresh Off the Boat: Stories of Immigration, Identity and Coming to America.* She is also a member of The Writers Grotto and frequently curates and participates in Bay Area literary readings with Seventeen Syllables, an Asian American writers collective. She is finishing "The Translator's Daughter," a memoir.

# Isthmus

**Marilyn Stablein**

I come to the island with food. I'm hiding. It's safe here. Father will come by boat. Soon.

Wood is plentiful. Logs soak until the bark loosens, falls off. Shiny trunks bake in the sun like the almonds Mother blanched and peeled before roasting. That bowl full of brown, discarded skins.

Matches dry in my pocket. I gather kindling, build a fire in my shelter. With my Buck Knife Father gave me, I whittle spear points on long sticks, build an arsenal of spears.

Last week, Father began packing his truck. "Why do I have to go?" I whined. "Can't I stay here?"

"Shut up! You can't wait here," Father said. "Do as I say." Dewdrops slid down his forehead. His wet T-shirt looked like a saggy dishtowel that hung in the kitchen too long. After Mother left, the dishtowels and T-shirts were always splotched. Mice crept into cupboards. She didn't want to leave. He made her.

They argued. Over money, over a leaky faucet, over runny eggs, moldy catsup, over me, the night business, the moored boat, the cargo, the take, the patrol.

Last summer, I pretended to be asleep, but the sound of their voices woke me. "You don't care about us," Mother cried. "We can't raise the boy on jail sentences."

"Lay off, Eleanor." He spat out "Eleanor" as if she were outside in the back shed, far away. "If you care so much, you take him."

"I always have."

"Go on. I'm not stopping you. Where you gonna go?"

"What's it to you? Why did I…ever…wait for you."

The cabin is near the island. I waited three weeks once. Father was jailed. No one knew where I was. When I came back from a long afternoon on the isthmus, I found Mother's note. "I'll come back," she wrote. Don't hide. Wait for me here!"

The tides are generous or forgetful. They croon and slather. Waves spit up shells like skulls, volcanoes, scissors, broken mugs. Water vomits garbage: plastic rope ends, sardine tins, fish carcass hopping with sand fleas, two ugly plastic bleach bottles that will never, ever corrode.

I walk. Up and down the beach. The path is wide but never boring or static like a mountain trail or cement sidewalk. At the tide line, every step is different. Water surges, buries my feet, then retreats. When the wave recedes, sand is sucked under my feet. Some gargling monster tongue slogs the shore.

Do beaches have sinkholes?

Driftwood fires the dark. The first night I set a can of chili in the coals to warm, then ate from the can with my knife.

I fall asleep counting the waves. The crash, soothing ripples, back and forth. My breath echoes. Just before Mother left, I nightraved and woke up swimming.

Mother tied the belt of her bathrobe tight when she burst into my room.

"What is it? What's the matter, honey? You cried out."

"Out?"

"Out! Cried out! What is it?" She shook me gently.

"I almost didn't make it."

"Make what?"

"We were sitting on the plaid tablecloth. On the beach. You sliced a huge watermelon into pieces. Red juice dribbled down Father's chin. Where he spit the seeds, ants landed on the white sand. No one saw the wave. Ants crawled over my arm, my hands, my face. Then water buried us."

"Did you drown?"

"I don't know. I met the wave head-on, dove up into it. Don't let a wave crash down on you. If you don't see it coming, you're dead."

This is not really an island. I walked here with my pack. When the tide takes a hike, I wade across shallow waves.

The spit is long, parallels the shore like an arm. With water on both sides, it feels like an island. Maybe the sands will shift and the gap between shore open up. For now, it connects.

I walk and walk and still the two waters, the two lands. Sometimes I meet a beachcomber; mostly I'm alone. Maybe the land bridges back to the mainland. If I walk far enough, I'll find out.

At night, I see the isthmus clearly. Like a bridge over a river. But if the isthmus connects land on two sides, I should feel secure or feel relief of some sort. But I don't.

What I like about the Kamikaze pilots in old black and white TV movies is their determination. How they confront their enemies head-on. That final burst of flame.

Father was in a war. He was wounded but healed. He returned when I was seven.

To kill time, I whittle. Small bark canoes cross the lagoon, reach the Great Barrier Reef. I like the way that sounds, Great Barrier Reef. The lagoon is warmer than the ocean. A spear I toss sidesteps a starfish.

In the morning, the first things: sounds of waves, seagulls, and the wind between the loosely piled slats of the shelter. Sand shakes out of my blanket.

A jar of peanut butter lasts a week. The loaf is history.

A spit is easy to spot from the air. It's a transgression, a misplaced wood shaving, a tail end drifting out so far it doesn't connect any longer. A trail of spittle on the frothy ocean chin. An afterthought, a flashback, an apostrophe at the end of a sentence.

A new morning. I know that sound. Father's boat cruises near shore! I run to the tide line. "Here. Over here,!" I yell and wave wildly.

The boat approaches. The motor stops. "Where's your father?" a gruff voice barks.

Not Father, his partner, that surly, stinky overweight creep. I hate him. My heart caves. I remember the hours they talked and laughed at the kitchen table after Father sent me to bed. The cabin is small; I hear everything.

"He's not with you?" I ask.

"Hell no, the bastard. He's not with me. Isn't he here?"

A burst pulls me down. I fall backward onto the sand. The echo chamber won't shut down. A blast clobbers me. The motor starts up again, much louder this time, grating like a chainsaw.

Lying on my back, I can't lift my head. I try again. My shoulder's killing me. My arm bleeds. Blood doesn't puddle like in the movies; it seeps into the sand. The sand is a sieve.

When I open my eyes, a woman mops my brow.

"He's stirring. Jake, bring the thermos!"

"What time is it?" I ask. Suddenly it's important to know this.

"Don't move," the woman says. "It's all right." Her head looms over me, shading my eyes from the midday sun. Her royal blue windbreaker inflates with wind, whips back and forth. She twists her scarf into a sling for my arm. "It's all right," she repeats.

She will take me home. I will sleep in sheets, walk her dog.

Home is fifty miles away. There is no dog. I heal.

Mother calls. The police tell her where I am. She comes to pick me up. She hugs me, cries.

"I was so worried, honey! I came back with the car. You were gone."

"I was hiding."

"Poor baby."

"I waited. Father said he'd come. I got shot. This woman came—"

"That's fine," she says. "Don't talk now. It's time to go."

Mother thanks the woman. We drive to a new place, a trailer this time. I go to school, but I'm older than the other kids. I missed some things: fractions, social studies, quizzes.

I still dream of the isthmus. I see it from above, the landmark of white between blue, tethering great masses of land, the great connector. Father will come. Soon.

---

**AUTHOR'S STATEMENT**

The genesis of this story was the setting. In a dream I saw the landscape far below me, as if I were a pilot looking down through a cockpit window though there was no window or plane in the dream. I wasn't aware of floating, gliding, or even effortlessly or unconsciously hovering in a cloudless, windless sky (a typical scenario in some flying dreams). Yet there I was. As my eyes gazed earthward, a long, narrow strip of sand surrounded by whitecapped ocean waves on two sides reached out like an arm and caught my attention.

In the story, a young boy leaves an uncertain homelife and bravely sets out on his own. As he walks along the shore of the isthmus, memories taunt him. Doubts arise as he tries to survive in a strange, harsh environment with only a buck knife and few supplies. As I began to write, I remembered that the most memorable strip of land I visited that reached out into the sea was Dungeness Spit, a five-mile-long, isthmus-like strip of sand projecting into the straits of San Juan de Fuca off the Olympic penninsula in Washington State.

The land and the boy's imagination are both vulnerable. A bleak starkness pervades. On a solo campout of sorts, he watches, explores, whittles, cooks, listens, dreams, frets, worries, and thinks about his life, his parents, the ocean, the environment. Physical hardships test personal endurance, bravery, and ingenuity. The temporary nomadic, solitary lifestyle may enhance or induce a spiritual or psychological awakening. His situation evokes an intentional, traditional coming-of-age ritual that a young man may encounter in many diverse traditions: an Aboriginal Australian on a walkabout; an arctic Inuit who goes off temporarily to live alone in an outcamp.

The bleak landscape of dried kelp and large drift logs, common on the beaches of Cascadia—stripped of bark, denuded, twisted, and bleached—cast an eerie pall but ultimately symbolize qualities of endurance, shelter, and survival.

Without attempting to interpret or explain how or why the story elements collide, evolve, and transform, I'll just say that as the story progresses, the ultimate impermanence of nature, life, consciousness, and memory weave back and forth, and in and out.

**MARILYN STABLEIN** is a poet, essayist, fiction writer, and mixed-media artist whose collages, assemblages, sculptural artist's books, and performance art explore and document visual narrative, travelogue, and memoir. Her recent books are *Vermin: A Traveler's Bestiary* (Spuyten Duyvil), *Houseboat on the Ganges & A Room in Kathmandu: Letters from India & Nepal 1966–1972* (Chin Music Press), and *Milepost 27: Poems* (Black Heron Press).

# Milestones

**Rebecca Thomas**

As I change my son, he quiets, turns,
and calls out. "You talking to your brother
on the other side of the wall?" I ask.
He is four months old. He doesn't yet know
where his brother sleeps or how far sound carries.
He has only begun to find power in his voice,
that he can call, and someone will come.
He doesn't yet know that states away children
are held in cages, in tents, in the Texas sun,
and sometimes crying brings no one.
Soon he will learn he is his own person,
and a thing can remain even when he leaves.
My son calms as he watches his shadow.
He doesn't yet know what separation means.

---

AUTHOR'S STATEMENT

My second son was born shortly before the Trump administration began the cruel practice of separating migrant children from their parents. At the time that the images and ProPublica tapes broke, he was just a few months old. As I nursed him each day and night, his body curled into mine, I would look at my phone and see the pictures of these children, hear their voices call for their parents, and read about babies being taken away from their mothers. I clutched my son closer.

As parents, we have the honor of watching our children become aware of the world, but as parents, we also witness our children beginning to understand the reality of the world. How do we raise children, especially boys, to be aware of this? How do we raise children, especially boys, to acknowledge their privilege, to make their voices heard for justice?

This poem was written as I was nursing. Writing while parenting young children is difficult. But during a feeding session, this poem came nearly complete. It raises questions I think all parents ask. How do we live in a world of such inequity? How do we teach our children about this? What if it was me? What if it was my sons?

REBECCA THOMAS is the editor of *Ms. Aligned 3;* her bio note is on page x.

# Dumaguete

**Marianne Villanueva**

When Carlos's mother decided to take him to Dumaguete, on the other side of the island, he didn't question her. One day she said, we have to go, and they did, walking with their overnight bags to the bus station, whose uneven ground was pooled with muddy brown water in which he could detect shapes darting, tiny black minnows. He stumbled once or twice but his mother never paused or looked behind her and he hurried to catch up.

He wondered why she hadn't asked the driver to take them. Nanding had returned home after dropping off Carlos's father at the office. But his mother had asked the security guard to call them a cab. The cab driver had stared at his mother as they got into the back. Carlos wanted to hit him.

His mother had dressed carefully for the trip. She was wearing one of her floaty dresses, and high-heeled white sandals, the better to show off her toes, which were long and thin and elegant and nothing like Carlos's, who in almost everything had taken after his father.

We are going to Seven Seas Resort, his mother said. You will like it. They have a pool.

And Carlos did like it, but that was only after he had thrown up twice during the twelve-hour bus ride along a twisty, narrow road that hugged the sides of the steep mountain. Whenever Carlos looked out the window, he saw terrifying views of deep, wooded gorges and, occasionally, the glint of flashing water. A sour vomit smell clogged his mouth, his nostrils, and Carlos was deeply embarrassed.

None of the other passengers seemed to mind. The old woman behind them even leaned forward and handed his mother a couple of plastic bags.

The town itself was small and not at all like what he'd expected. There were no signal lights and everyone rode around on motorbikes or tricycles. These roamed all over the city and made a terrific, belching noise. Smoke poured from their exhaust pipes, marring the fresh air that blew in from the ocean.

One day, they visited a crocodile farm. Carlos was intrigued by the scaly creatures whose mouths opened astonishingly wide at the approach, as though manipulated by invisible hinges.

Another day, they visited a large zoo near the central plaza. His mother walked around silently, apparently content, her eyes resting briefly on the animals in their cages, one said to be the *tamaraw*, a horned beast that looked, to Carlos, like nothing so much as a very small water buffalo, with a black hide and two thick, curving horns.

On the fourth day, Carlos felt his insides contract. His mother had taken him to the green campus of Silliman University. There, among the tall, old acacia trees, they'd stumbled across a small museum that held shells and voodoo charms from another small island, a short boat ride away: Siquijor, whose faint outline was just visible from Dumaguete's seaside promenade. All day, outrigger canoes transporting shells for selling to tourists plied the distance between the two islands. For years, Carlos had heard stories about this island, but his mother showed no inclination to go there.

Back home, his *yaya*, Dulce, had told him about witches, about the *manunungod* who hides under the floor of the room of a sick person, causing the patient to toss and turn feverishly. She had told him about *aswang*, creatures with long tongues who suck babies from the stomachs of pregnant women.

Dulce slept on a straw mat on the floor of his room. She only told him these stories when it was late and she was sure Carlos's father was asleep. Looking at the blackened implements in the Silliman museum, he was suddenly reminded of the *yaya* and of her strangely urgent whisperings. And almost at the same instant, a picture of his room rose up in his memory: the Matchbox cars neatly arranged on the shelves, the navy blue bedspread. Ma, he said, quite without thinking, I miss Papa.

Shush, his mother said. Stop being such a baby.

Will I ever see him again, Carlos asked, and to his horror tears began to well up in his eyes.

Of course you will, his mother said, patting his shoulder. Her hand was cool. He could feel the imprint of its coolness on the back of his T-shirt. It felt good.

Of course you will, his mother repeated, looking intently into his eyes. And Carlos was once again caught in that gaze, that green-eyed gaze that seemed to speak of nothing so much as time and sadness. He didn't know why his mother should have green eyes, when all his classmates' mothers had brown; why she didn't seem to love his father and threatened to leave him after every argument.

This was the first time she had taken him with her, though. Carlos had expected they would catch the next flight to Manila, where his grandparents lived. But instead his mother had taken him to this strange city where they knew no one.

On the fifth or sixth day, a change seemed to come over his mother. Alert as he was to her ever-shifting moods, he sensed the change in her almost immediately. She seemed distracted, found excuses to leave him and go to the hotel lobby. Once, when he was swimming in the pool, he looked up and she was no longer in the deck chair that she'd dragged over to the shallow end, where he could look up from time to time and watch her reading her book *(A Journey of One Hundred Years*—what kind of title was that? It was not a book he would ever want to read.) When his mother was reading, two deep lines appeared on either side of her mouth, and she didn't look pretty anymore. For that reason, Carlos tried to call out to her and distract her, splashing energetically and making sure a few drops of water landed on her still form.

Now, when he looked up, she was gone. He felt a familiar panic rising. He feared she had left the hotel, that she might even have left the city. Now, Carlos was sure he was all alone. Now he must get his things and find his way back to his father, who lived all the way on the other side of the island.

Two days before, a group of men had come to stay at the hotel. They were large, stout men, with leathery skin and loud voices. They made the waitresses bring tray after tray of beer. They sat hunched over their restaurant table, telling stories about women and laughing.

It was the thought of these recent visitors that made Carlos finally get out of the pool, almost tripping over his towel in his haste. He noticed his mother had left her book, face down, on the ground beside the deck chair. One of the stout men who had arrived a few nights ago was sunning himself on a towel, some distance away. Carlos couldn't be sure, but he felt that the man had been watching him. This angered him; he tried to stare the man down, which was difficult since the man was wearing shades that reflected a deep, bronze sheen.

Carlos picked up his mother's book—he felt sure that the man would paw through it otherwise—and hurried to the cottage he and his mother shared, set some way back from the pool. He stepped on the veranda and noticed that his mother's slippers were gone. He opened the door to their room—by this time everything was swimming painfully in his head and he had a headache and a whoosh of cold air from the air conditioner disconcerted him. The room was frigid. The beds were as they had been when he and his mother had left that morning, bringing their towels and their sunblock and her book. He went to the bathroom and saw her toiletries—brush, perfume bottle, lipstick—arranged neatly on the right side of the vanity. His mother had been laughing that morning, she had been happy. But Carlos had not returned her gaiety. He had remained silent in response to all her jibing.

He flipped the light on. In the harsh, fluorescent glare, he saw himself in the mirror. Who was this stranger peering back at him with a frightened expression? It was certainly not he, for he always felt he knew how to hide his emotions. It was a skill his mother lacked, and he had realized this about her very early. And he had carefully tended to his face, even when he was startled, even when he felt lost.

Now, however, the mirror made him call out.

Ma, he said. And then, more strongly, Ma!

He was aware that his own mother could not hear him, that she was faraway, and he realized, with frightening clarity, that he was nothing but a child. He had loved it when, on his ninth birthday, almost a year ago, his father had surprised him with a party. It had been wonderful, for his mother had worn a white dress and held his father's hand and they had talked to each other in loving tones.

His mother had gone away for a much longer time than usual, and Carlos felt her absence much more keenly. He felt adrift. His father would sneer hatefully at him. Your mother is not coming back.

The days would pass in a long string of waiting.

Another woman would come by the house. She had a deep, throaty laugh and wore colorful, high-heeled shoes that matched whatever dress she happened to be wearing.

The other woman's name, he found out, was Rica. Her husband, Carlos learned from his *yaya,* who seemed angry at the woman and even angrier at Carlos's father, had moved to the States and was living with another woman there. He had taken Rica's two young sons with him. Now, Rica had no one—no one, that is, except for Carlos's father.

"Your father is a prince," Rica had said once to Carlos. In response, Carlos had merely shrugged.

Carlos dreamt of writing her a note, telling her to follow her husband, but he feared provoking his father's wrath. Instead, he waited, pleading with his mother in his thoughts. And, each time, it seemed that his mother did hear him, because from whatever place she happened to be, Carlos's mother would return. He would come down to breakfast one day and see her sitting demurely at the table, her hair damp and smelling clean and fresh, as if she had lingered among flowers. It was only then, at the moment of her return, that Carlos knew his heart had been broken. The pain was so real that he found it impossible to eat. It was as if his father and his mother had each taken knives and plunged them into his very being. He, the CENTER of these two opposing forces, could scarcely move and wanted only to die from exhaustion, the exhaustion of loving two people who felt only bitterness.

Carlos would often ask himself why his mother and father could not be happy. Or even *pretend* to be happy, for his sake. He dreamt that Rica assumed the shape of a fantastic, plumed bird. In her outstretched wings, she cradled his father's sleeping form. Other times, he dreamt of his mother, or at least of a being he felt to be his mother, though this woman was stooped and had white hair. In his dreams, his fragile, old mother moved about restlessly, tapping the floors with a wooden cane and then bending low as if listening for a sound from under the floorboards. Once, she lifted it and hit a boy lurking in the shadows. Carlos cried out and felt pain shoot up his right arm. When he woke in the morning, the inside of his right elbow was bruised. Perhaps, he mused, he was a shapeshifter who visited others in his dreams.

The only thing that made Carlos feel better, after having had such a dream, was the voice of his *yaya*. Carlos didn't know how old Dulce was, but she was very old. She had come to the family with Carlos's mother. When Carlos's mother was not around, it was Dulce who talked to him, and told him stories at night, and made sure he ate his dinner. Sometimes Olivia looked at him and shook her head sadly. Then Carlos wondered what he had done. He dreamed of his mother, always.

Once, his mother told him she had been in Costa Rica. He had felt anguish at this knowledge, at the wounding thought that his mother had boarded a plane, that she had flown many thousands of miles away from him, without a second thought.

He finally asked her what she enjoyed most (when all the while he needed all the force of his will to tamp down his anger) and she had said, "The birds."

She then talked about the scenery, and how long it had taken to get to this beach and that, and how she was finally able to practice her Spanish, which had grown rusty from disuse. She described the friendliness of the people, their lustrous eyes and brown skin. The food, too, she had fallen in love with—the *callo pinto*—rice and black beans—with every meal; the fat, juicy watermelons, the papayas, the piña, the fried plantains; the grilled chicken; the picadillo de chayote with cilantro; and her inn, which was on some street whose name she couldn't remember but which was only a block away from the Ministry of Tourism. His mother said she loved the way everyone would say, *"No te preoccupe,"* which was now her favourite expression.

And, while his mother was describing all these things for him—she had no pictures, she never took a camera anywhere—Carlos too began to see in his mind the beautiful, clean country and the smiling, unworried people. He thought it must be like paradise, where he expected to go one day, and even though some part of him knew that his mother could not be trusted, that some of what she was telling him was not absolutely real, he understood why she had chosen to leave out details here and there. The world was a messy place that his mother wanted no part of. But here, with Carlos, she had invented an idea of a place where it was possible to be perfectly happy. The invention would always be their secret, a gift she shared only with Carlos.

He did not ask her whether she had told anyone that she was married and had a son. He guessed that his mother might not want to offer this information, not willingly. And anyway she was over *there,* where no one knew her and where she must have felt she could start afresh. It was cruel, then, of him to have called her back, though he had had to do it; he simply couldn't live without her.

As Carlos left the frigid room and headed towards the main building, he had to skirt a grove of coconut trees, and he noticed for the first time that he had seen no birds in this place, and he wondered whether it might be possible for him one day to see Costa Rica, his mother's beautiful paradise, for himself.

The men were loud tonight. He could hear them, laughing and talking in the restaurant. The waitresses scurried around with frightened faces. The loudest of the men was puffing on a big cigar. He wore dark glasses, even in the gloom of the restaurant. He had a pistol tucked against his bulging stomach, in the waistband of his tight khaki pants. The others called him "Sir."

Carlos could feel Sir watching him as he entered the restaurant. Perhaps he'd been watching him a long time already. It was hard to tell, behind the opaque glasses. Carlos skirted his table carefully, but a heavy, dark hand shot out and Carlos, feeling the heavy pressure against his chest, stopped.

"*Teka muna,*" the man said. He was smiling. "I want to ask you something." Carlos noticed the flash of gold on one of his teeth.

Sir stretched out the hand that held the cigar, pointing at Carlos's mouth. "Try! Try!" he kept saying.

Carlos shook his head. He wished he could pretend he was deaf-mute. He'd done this, sometimes, and sometimes it had worked. Sometimes, when his teachers asked him a question he didn't know how to answer, he rolled his eyes and stuck out his tongue. This made his math teacher, in particular, increasingly angry. Finally the teacher had thrown a blackboard eraser at him and ordered him out of the classroom. Carlos had moved slowly among the desks, as if underwater.

His mother didn't know, and he'd make sure she never knew, that in the last year he had learned how to smoke, filching a cigarette a week from the packs his father left on his dresser. He would take the precious stick to a secluded spot in their garden where, hidden behind a large *balete* tree, he would light it and practice breathing slowly, in and out, watching the smoke curl luxuriantly in the air above him. Sometimes he would deepen his voice and imitate his father. It made him feel big and proud to walk with his head held high and cocked to one side, the cigarette dangling from a corner of his mouth. Sometimes Carlos imagined it was *he* who held Rica, he who Rica gazed at with longing. And he could hardly wait until the day when he, too, could buy presents for pretty women and make them laugh.

Sir kept his paw against Carlos's thin chest, and suddenly Carlos felt like crying. He turned his head, looking around for his mother, and Sir said, "Where is she?"

Carlos shrugged.

"The two of you come here by yourselves?" Sir asked. "Where is your father?" He pronounced it Pa-DERR; it was clear to Carlos that Sir was not an educated man. But this knowledge only increased his unease, and he flushed bright red. Then, he raised his shoulders and shrugged, miming an *I don't know*.

He raised both palms to the air. A hiccup of fear rose to his throat and before he could stop it, it emerged sounding like a belch. Sir laughed.

"What happened to you, *ha,* boy? I hear you talking to your mom so I know you're not deaf or dumb. Maybe just scared, *ha?* Scared of Mario?"

Carlos mimed again, desperately rolling his eyes and shrugging. Sir stopped laughing and gazed at him through narrowed eyes. He'd tired of the game, Carlos could feel it, but he didn't know what else to do. He stood there, waiting.

Sir gave him a slight push, and Carlos, off balance, stumbled. Sir laughed, and the other men laughed, too. Carlos's face was burning. He faced the men.

"My father is coming," Carlos said. "He is coming."

But saying these words caused a kind of panic to rise in him. He realized, for the first time, that they really were alone there, he and his mother. He wondered why they were there at all, in that place so far from home, surrounded by strangers. And he wondered why his father had let them go, why his father was always letting them go, why he was never around at the moment of Carlos's greatest need. Such as now.

Perhaps it was the woman in the red dress, the one who came over when Carlos's mother was away. Perhaps she was the cause of his mother's unhappiness and ruin.

As he walked away, forcing himself to move slowly, Carlos heard Sir saying something to the others. He caught the word *puki* and the evil in their laughter. His heart was racing by the time he reached their cottage.

He flung open the door. His mother was on the bed, doing a crossword puzzle. She was wearing a loose, blue shift, and her hair was tied back from her face in a ponytail. She looked fresh and rested. She looked up when he entered and smiled.

"Where were you?" she said, as if she had been sitting there all this time.

Carlos sat on the bed.

"I want to go home," he said. He meant, *I want to go to my father.* She knew that was what he meant. Her face grew cold.

"No, not yet," she said. After a moment, she continued, "Aren't you having fun here? The food is good, no? I saw you eat so many mangos this morning."

"I don't care about mangos!" Carlos suddenly screamed.

His mother's arms encircled him almost immediately, but he would not be comforted. "You. Think. I. Care. About. Mangos!" He screamed and screamed. Spittle came out of his mouth. His mother continued to hold him. Eventually, his screams subsided to a loud sobbing. He became still, listening to his mother's soft voice. "Shhh, shhh, shhh," she said. "You're tired. Just tired."

Carlos closed his eyes. He lay in his mother's arms, exhausted.

He decided he could not tell her about the men in the restaurant. He would think up some excuse to prevent her from leaving the room. Perhaps he'd say he wasn't feeling well. He'd lie still and listless on the bed, listening to her low, soothing voice. He'd even force tears from his eyes, so many that they would stain the front of her dress. He'd find a way to hold her with him, there.

And then, in two days—it would only be as long as that, he was sure—his father would come and fetch them. He would wrap his arms around Carlos and say, You've had an adventure. Wasn't it fun?

---

**AUTHOR'S STATEMENT**

When I was twenty-one, I started my master's degree in East Asian Studies (concentration in Chinese) at Stanford University. It seems strange now—to go West to study about the East—but I wanted to go abroad, like everyone in my family had done (my parents, my older sister). Because I was more interested in the East than about anything else, I thought this would be a good compromise.

The summer between my first and second year in East Asian Studies, I took a creative writing workshop from John L'Heureux, who was the director of the creative writing program. He told me I should apply for the program—a suggestion that came out of the blue, but was nice. I decided, just like that, to apply. I was accepted, and that's why I'm a writer today.

By the time I wrote "Dumaguete," I'd been writing pretty steadily. I had a whole cache of stories that I'd built up over decades. I'd keep them on my computer and only send them out sporadically: I was a mom, I moved in and out of apartments and houses, I worked as an administrator and as a teacher. But I would get up at four every morning and write for at least two hours.

When I wrote "Dumaguete," my son was in grade school. I'd taken him and my niece to visit Dumaguete. Everything in the story comes from that trip. It was a beautiful, beautiful time in my life: to be a mother and a writer—that was the most joyous feeling.

The mother in the story is not happy, which is where the story deviates from my experience. But I wanted to capture the feeling of a marriage that was more about power and control than it was about partnership. There are many marriages like that, in all parts of the world, and the wives generally get the worst of it. I also felt that the boy in the story is as much a victim as his mother. To be in the midst of two opposing forces is to be split apart.

Bad marriages are devastating to children. The boy in "Dumaguete" is very sensitive and very alive to his mother's moods. That's why it is so painful for him to watch her.

After I reread the story, my heart went out to the son. What will he be? How will he survive? These are questions I left for readers to figure out for themselves.

**MARIANNE VILLANUEVA** was born and raised in the Philippines. She is the author of the short-story collections *Ginseng and Other Tales from Manila, Mayor of the Roses,* and *The Lost Language.* Her novella, *Jenalyn,* was a 2014 finalist for the UK's Saboteur Award. Her individual stories have been finalists for the O. Henry Literature Prize, nominated for the Pushcart, and included in Wigleaf's Top 50 (very) short fiction of 2016.

# About the Artists

**MELISSA CHIMERA** is a conservationist and Honolulu native of Lebanese and Filipino ancestry. Her work investigates species extinction, globalization and human migration and has been exhibited worldwide, with solo shows such as *Migrant* at the Honolulu Museum of Art and *Agents of Change* at the Hui No'eau Visual Arts Center, Maui. Her most recent project as artist and curator is *The Far Shore: Navigating Homelands* for the Arab American National Museum. The exhibition of contemporary art and poetry concerns a highly politicized issue—Arab immigration to America—viewed through the lens of the personal and familial. She is the recipient of the Catherine E. B. Cox Award and has been named as a finalist for the 2019 Lange-Taylor Prize, Duke University Documentary Studies. She keeps a studio on Hawai'i Island, where she lives with her husband and son. (Above photograph by Marie Hobro.)

In *Old Country, Syria,* the painting selected for the front cover of this volume, she traces her Lebanese ancestry in a family tree where a postcard written from her grandfather, Nash Ne Jame, to his only surviving brother after World War I, uses the term "old country." WWI claimed five out of eight immediate family members, and while significantly traumatic to Ne Jame's youth, his pre-American life was a subject he never discussed, leaving the artist to piece together a family history through documents and photographs.

**CARLY ELIZABETH HUGGINS** grew up driving around South Florida, making her way from Naples to West Palm Beach. She works in multiple media, including paint on canvas and jewelry. She finds inspiration in reflection and through the fluidity of nature and music. After years of living in West Virginia, she recently moved with her husband and son to Fort Myers, Florida.

Of her work, she writes, "My journey with art began as a child. Growing up in South Florida, I was always surrounded by ocean life, flowers, and bright tropical palm trees. Little did I know that my path would lead me to my home here, in the wild, wonderful West Virginia. My love for water and nature continues to grow, with every mystical river, mountain laurel, and moonrise over our rolling green hills, as this is a strong source of inspiration for me."

Of the painting selected for the back cover of this volume, she says, "I have always had a passion for the abstract, yet shortly after becoming a mother, I found myself being drawn to less defined images. *Hurricane* is part of a series of paintings I created when I was trying to find a space for myself as a new mother. It evolved from an old image I kept exploring: an eye blossoming with petals. I found myself letting go of that image and releasing control. *Hurricane* was for me."

Made in USA - Kendallville, IN
1058996_9780979950421
03.20.2020 1615